"Morning by morning new mercies I see...."

— From "Great Is Thy Faithfulness,"
Thomas O. Chisholm, 1923

Other books by Stan Purdum

Roll Around Heaven All Day

Playing In Traffic

New Mercies I See

by
Stan Purdum

CSS Publishing Company, Inc., Lima, Ohio

NEW MERCIES I SEE

"Night Trek" was previously published serially in *Vital Christianity*, January and Febru-
ary 1989.

A drama version of "Spring Story" was published in *Drama Ministry*, January-February,
1998.

"Still Standing" was published in *The War Cry*, July 7, 2001.

Library of Congress Cataloging-in-Publication Data

Purdum, Stan, 1945-
  New mercies I see / by Stan Purdum.
    p. cm.
  ISBN 0-7880-1958-9 (pbk. : alk. paper)
  1. Rural churches—Fiction. 2. Christian fiction, American. I. Title.
  PS3616.U73 N49 2003
  813'.6—dc21

                                                              2002152669

Cover illustration by Chris Patton.

For more information about CSS Publishing Company resources, visit our website at
www.csspub.com or e-mail us at custserv@csspub.com or call (800) 241-4056.

ISBN 0-7880-1958-9   PRINTED IN U.S.A.

Contents

1. A Fair Hearing

From the look on Delores' face as she strode up our walk, I knew that, once again, my sermon hadn't sat well with her.

We'd just gotten home from church when the sound of a car in the driveway made me look out the window. "You might want to hold off putting dinner on the table, Susie," I said. "Delores is here."

My normally patient mate groaned. "Why does it always have to be right after church? Doesn't that woman's family expect her home?"

"Evidently not right away," I said, resignedly. Hearing the knock, I pasted on a smile and answered the door. "Hello, Delores."

"I need a word, Reverend Payton," the stocky woman said.

"I thought perhaps that was the case." I stood aside for Delores to enter and waved her toward a chair in the living room.

She began without preliminaries. "About what you said about that text this morning, Reverend, you surely weren't right. It means ..."

While Delores forged on, I listened as best I could, but by now, she had disagreed with me so often that I pretty well knew what she was going to say. Although Delores had always attended the little Methodist Church I now pastored, she really wasn't a Methodist at heart. A few years before my arrival in Thornberry, Delores had gone to a revival tent meeting led by a freelance evangelist who espoused a theology far to the right of the Christian mainstream. She had gotten caught up in the revival and now considered it her mission to move our congregation to the theological position of the evangelist, a direction I was not inclined to support.

Delores was clearly following her same line of argument again, and despite my best efforts to stay with her, the aroma of beef gravy emanating from our kitchen kept distracting me.

For me, Sunday noon always felt like the end of the week. Much of what I did throughout the preceding six days aimed toward Sunday morning. I enjoyed preaching, and I approached the whole Sunday service with high energy. But once the service was over, I felt as drained as a battery that's been used to jumpstart a whole fleet of cars. I'd given my all, and I was always famished. Susie usually put a beef roast — one of my favorite meals — in the oven before we left for the service, so that it would be ready on our arrival home. This week's roast now beckoned me, but Delores was not about to release me yet to enjoy it.

Despite her bluntness and tenacity, Delores was not a mean-spirited person. In fact, she was someone I could count on to help with church activities. She gave generously to the programs of the church and rarely missed a service.

Ironically, despite her self-imposed objective to "save" our congregation, her own family did not attend church with her. Her husband spent his weekends in his garage, tinkering with the old cars he loved restoring. The couple's teenage son, Ben, was often there with his father. The pair of them came to church with Delores on Christmas Eve, but rarely at any other time. Thus far, I had resisted the temptation to suggest that Delores aim her evangelism efforts at her own family. But today, the thought of the hot crescent rolls in our kitchen turning cold before I could get to them reawakened the notion.

Thinking better of it, I suppressed the urge and forced my attention back to what Delores was saying. Mercifully, she seemed to be winding down. When she stopped, I said, "But, as you know, what you are suggesting really isn't where either the Methodist Church or I myself am at on this matter." I went on to restate the central theme of that morning's sermon.

"But —"

"I do want to thank you for telling me what you think about this, however," I said. "If you'd like to talk further, perhaps you could call and we could set up an appointment."

"Well, I guess that isn't necessary, as long as you've understood what I've said." She rose to her feet as she spoke, partly because I was exerting upward pressure on her elbow.

"I have," I assured her. "Thank you for coming." I steered her toward the door.

When she was gone, I rushed to the kitchen, where Susie was putting the food on the table.

"Delores is certainly persistent," Susie said once we'd started eating. "She really believes things her way."

"She does, and she's sincere. But if she didn't feel so powerless to mold her family into what she wants it to be, she might not be so determined to influence the church."

"Got her all figured out, huh, Tom?" Susie was grinning.

"Okay, so maybe I'm playing psychiatrist here, but it makes sense."

Over the next year and a half or so, Delores accosted me perhaps a dozen times more with variations on her theme. I began to think of her as the "loyal opposition" who labored faithfully within an environment she hoped to change.

But in time, my intransigence became too much for her. Following a Sunday service in late January, she stayed behind to tell me that she'd decided to transfer her membership to a church in the next town. She named the congregation, one independent of any denomination. From what I knew of it, I assumed it would be more in line with her beliefs. While I was sincerely sorry to lose Delores from our congregation, and told her so, I gave her my blessing.

From that point on, Delores attended no more services at our church. Of course, she still lived in tiny Thornberry, so I saw her around the community. She was always friendly — even jovial — and made no mention of our theological disagreements. We had a few social conversations, and when our first child, Tommy, was born, Delores sent a congratulations card.

And so it went for a couple of years. Then, on a Thursday evening in late spring, Delores pulled into the parsonage driveway. Through the window, I watched her approach the house, and I was struck that her demeanor was different. Where before she had marched purposely up my walk, she now moved with hesitation, as if she were unsure or uneasy about her reason for visiting.

I met her at the door.

"Could I talk to you?" she asked quietly.

"Of course. Come in."

She sat down heavily and I took the chair opposite her.

"Ben has gotten himself into some trouble," she said. "A grocery store holdup. He's in the county jail."

"I'm so sorry. What can I do to help?"

Tears were running down Delores' cheeks, and she continued as if she had not heard me. "We didn't bring him up that way; I don't know why he ..." At that point she began sobbing.

I reached out and touched Delores' hand. "This must be terrible for you," I said.

She dabbed her eyes with a hankie. "Ben is 19 now, you know. He's not a juvenile anymore. He'll be tried as an adult."

"That is serious," I said. And then I waited. I still had no clear idea why Delores had come to me.

The silence stretched between us, broken only by Delores' sighs as she struggled to regain her composure. Finally she said, "I was wondering if you'd go see Ben. He's in the jail, but I think they'll let a minister talk to him."

"Yes, of course."

"I know I'm not a member here anymore, but —"

"That doesn't matter. I'll go over yet this evening."

"Oh, thank you. I think he needs someone to talk to. His father's too angry and well, he's never seemed to listen to me real good."

After Delores left, I ran upstairs to tell Susie where I was going.

"I wonder why she asked you to go instead of her own minister," Susie mused.

"I don't know. Anyway, I'm heading over now to see Ben."

At the jail, I found a very frightened and chastened Ben, who indeed did want someone to talk to. I visited him that evening and a few more times throughout the trial process, and then several times during the year he spent incarcerated after he was found guilty.

Upon his release, Ben moved to Fremont where he lived briefly with an uncle while he got himself established. He soon had a job as a mechanic in a Chevy garage, and he was staying out of trouble.

Delores continued to attend the other church, but she stopped by our house one day shortly after it was announced that the bishop had appointed me to the North Doncaster parish and that I would be leaving Thornberry. "I'm sorry to see you leave," she said.

"Thanks, Delores. I'll miss Thornberry and the folks here. What do you hear from Ben?"

She smiled. "Oh, he's just been promoted. He's going to be a service manager. They're sending him to a certification program and everything."

"I'm glad he's doing so well."

"Yes, and I want to thank you again for all you did for him. I guess I should have asked my minister to go to Ben, but, well, I was afraid he'd be so intent on saving Ben's soul that he wouldn't really listen to him. I knew you'd give Ben a fair hearing."

2. Board Action

Charlie Redgate shook his head and said, "Your mistake was asking in the first place."

"You don't see the importance of a private line?" I said, surprised.

"Oh, but I do. Your mistake was *asking*. Some things you should just do without getting permission."

Charlie had been a minister for nearly 40 years, and he currently pastored the Methodist Church in a county seat town not far from Thornberry. Since I was new to the ministry, my district superintendent had assigned Charlie as a kind of mentor to help me through the first year. We had lunch together about once a month.

I had just told Charlie the tale of my latest frustration — the attempt to get the party phone line in my parsonage replaced with a private line. When I first arrived at Thornberry, I was surprised to find that party lines were still in use in our county. But this part of Ohio was rural and served by a small phone company. Private lines were available, but at higher cost, and party lines were still common in the area. The parsonage was on a three-party line, and for reasons that escaped me, my predecessor had never requested that this arrangement be changed.

The three-party line meant that often, when I picked up the phone to make an outgoing call, the line was already in use. Courtesy dictated that I hang up immediately so as not to overhear the conversation on the line. The multi-party line also meant that when I was using the phone, one or both of the other users was likely to pick it up. Normally, they too would hang up quickly, but sometimes, especially if my call went on for more than a few minutes, one of the other parties would pick the phone up every minute or so, not so subtly communicating that he or she wanted the line and pressuring me to draw my conversation to a quick close.

Even more problematic was that those calling me often got a busy signal, an annoyance most of the time but a real problem when the call was urgent. Then, too, callers were reluctant to discuss personal matters on the phone since there was no guarantee that our conversation would not be overheard.

13

I was convinced we needed a private phone line in the parsonage.

Because the phone was part of the package provided for the pastor by the church, I assumed that changing the setup required the approval of a church committee.

But which one? Although the Methodist system provided for a standard set of committees in each congregation, local practice often dictated which committees actually made which decisions. The overall decision-making body, however, was the Official Board, and I started there. The discussion, as I'd just recounted for Charlie, went like this:

Me: "I'd like to request that we change the parsonage phone to a private line." I went on to state the reasons.

Board member A: "That's sounds reasonable. I've had trouble getting through to the pastor myself a few times."

Board member B: "I agree. The pastor should have a private line."

Board member C: "How much will it cost?"

Me: "I've checked with the phone company. It will be $2.30 more per month."

Board member B: "That's manageable."

Board member C: "But isn't the phone related to the property? Don't the trustees have to make this decision?"

Board member A: "Maybe you're right."

Board chairman: "All right. We'll refer the matter to the trustees." Then turning to the trustee who represented that body on the Official Board, the chairman said, "Don, will you convey this to the next meeting of the trustees?"

Don: (appearing surprised) "I don't know. This sounds like a board decision to me. But okay, I'll take it to the trustees."

The trustees were responsible for making sure the church building and grounds were cared for and for managing any endowment monies. The Thornberry church, thanks to the largess of several now-deceased members, had a tidy endowment fund. The trustees used the interest from the fund to pay for repairs, maintenance, and improvements.

As in most congregations in those days, Thornberry's board of trustees was comprised totally of men. Although no rule said that

14

women couldn't serve as trustees, men were usually nominated on the assumption that they could actually do some of the repair and maintenance work themselves. In rural and small town congregations especially, trustees tended to be hands-on types who were comfortable wielding hand tools and paintbrushes.

The possession of these talents, I was soon to discover, didn't necessarily make them decisive in matters related to the church's money.

The next meeting of the trustees didn't take place until nearly a month after the Official Board meeting, and so Susie and I had continued to put up with the party line in the meantime. At the meeting, Don, true to his assignment, presented the case for the private line. He raised the matter right after the trustees had just voted to spend $13,500 to repave the church parking lot.

Trustee A: "Isn't this a matter for the Official Board?"
Don: "That's what I thought, but they referred it to us."
Trustee B: "How much is it?"
Don: "$2.30 a month."
Trustee A: "I don't know. We just spent a lot of money."
Don: "We did, but the phone costs won't come out of the endowment. That would be a regular operating cost. It would come out of the general budget."
Trustee A: "Which makes it an Official Board matter."
Trustee chairman: "But it's been referred to us. Does anyone want to make a motion on this?"
General silence.
Trustee chairman: (turning to me) "I guess we'd better hold off on the private line for now."

I went home flabbergasted, which was how I still felt when I met Charlie for lunch a few days later. "The group had just spent thousands for the blacktopping without flinching but quailed at the idea of adding a little over $2 to the monthly operating costs!" I fumed.

That's when Charlie told me I shouldn't have asked.

"But they're footing the bill for my phone," I said. "I thought I needed their consent."

15

"For some reason, church boards can lose perspective when asked to deal with small-expense items where they can't actually see the need. Your trustees could easily spend the money for paving because they see the broken blacktop every time they come to church. But with minor requests where they can't see the need, they can get all tangled up."

Charlie continued, "In my first church appointment, the parsonage needed several repairs. I was able to handle them, but I needed the church to pay for the materials. I soon found out that asking them to consider each small expense bogged them down in endless debates. But then I discovered that if I simply went to the hardware store and charged what I needed to the church's account, the bills were paid without discussion."

"Isn't that dangerous? Spending a church's money without the board's permission?"

"It was never a problem. As the pastor, you have some leeway for spending, but most churches never spell it out. Of course, for larger expenses, I'd get the board's agreement. In those cases, you have to make sure they can clearly see the need."

I went home a wiser man.

As it happened, the phone matter was resolved at the very next meeting of the Official Board. A few days before the board met, I got a phone call in midmorning from Keith Johnson, a church member in his fifties. "Thank God I finally got through," he said. "My granddaughter fell off the top of the slide in the schoolyard. She's hurt pretty bad — a head injury. We're here at the hospital with her. Can you come?"

I drove to the hospital immediately where I sat and prayed with the family while the little girl underwent surgery. And I rejoiced with them when the surgeon finally came out and informed them that she would make a full recovery.

During the time we were waiting, Keith mentioned that he had tried to call me several times, but kept getting a busy signal.

"I wasn't on the phone," I explained. "The parsonage is on a party line."

Keith looked surprised. "In this day and age?" he asked. "That won't do."

16

When the Official Board next met, Keith was there. He heard Don's report that the trustees had taken no action on the phone line. Keith immediately spoke up. "We've got to change that right away," he said. He went on to explain the difficulty he'd had reaching me. His account caused an immediate mood shift among the board members and the change was authorized at once. I called the phone company the next day to schedule the switchover to a private line.

That was the year the entire Methodist denomination merged with the Evangelical United Brethren and we all became "United Methodists." The main effect of the change locally was that the new organization dictated a renaming of the standing committees of the church, and the old Official Board was now the "Administrative Board." The new denomination also issued a fresh hymnbook.

The previous edition, the one in the Thornberry pews, had been published more than 40 years earlier. I hoped our congregation would decide to get the new hymnals, not only because many of our existing copies were worn out, but because this latest release contained some newer songs and updated liturgies. But when I mentioned the new hymnal to various members informally, I discovered that most were unconvinced that we needed it. I wasn't eager to be the lone champion for the purchase. And since the cost of new hymnals would be substantial, there was no way I could act without board approval.

The idea of what to do hit me the day before a scheduled Administrative Board meeting, and I set about making preparations.

The next evening when the members of the board arrived, they took their places, as usual, in a semicircle of chairs facing the board chairman. He was seated at a table, and directly to the left of the table, in plain view, stood a stack of our hymnals. I had left the best copies in the pews; this pile contained every hymnal with a broken spine, those with loose pages sticking out, the ones with stained and torn covers, and others with obvious damage.

As I'd planned, I said nothing at all about these hymnals, but several times during the meeting, I noticed various members eyeing the sorry-looking volumes in the stack. In about 90 minutes, we completed the items on the printed agenda. Finally, the chairman asked, "Is there anything else to come before the board?"

Mel Morley raised his hand. "I've been thinking. It's about time we replaced our hymnbooks." Several others nodded their agreement.

Five minutes later, after only minimal discussion, the motion had been passed to purchase the new hymnals. We placed the order the next morning.

3. Pioneers

Susie and I had both grown up in cities, so our move to Thornberry, a township 30 miles from the nearest population center, was our first experience with rural life, and we arrived feeling like pioneers. The parsonage had a large backyard, so during our first springtime there, we planted a vegetable garden. Though we'd had no experience at gardening, our parishioners were generous with advice, and before long, I carried the first basket load of green beans — triumphantly — into our kitchen. Again relying on advice from church members, we canned the beans for use during the coming winter. I felt proud that we were beginning to live off the land.

And so we progressed through the growing season, processing in turn, corn, a second crop of beans, carrots, potatoes, tomatoes, and squash. Along the way we learned which to can, which to freeze, and which simply to enjoy fresh.

By the end of summer, I was duly impressed with what we'd accomplished, and decided — without benefit of advice — to add a nut harvest to our larder. The source, I calculated, would be a large black-walnut tree growing in the parsonage yard. I'd heard that walnut trees do not yield a crop every year, but I could see green globes forming in the branches as fall approached, and I realized that this would indeed be a nut-bearing year. I waited eagerly for the crop to fall from the high branches.

By early October, the walnuts, each encased in a tough green husk as large as a baseball, had begun dropping to the ground beneath the tree.

In the church, the first Sunday of October has long been designated as "Worldwide Communion Sunday," a day on which, as a show of unity, Christian denominations around the planet participate in Holy Communion. Like most Methodist churches, the congregation at Thornberry offered the Sacrament only bimonthly. Sundays when it occurred were regarded as special, and the Sunday for Worldwide Communion was preeminent. I always took extra care with my sermon for that day, and made sure all the arrangements for the Communion service itself were in place.

On the Saturday before the first Sunday that October, I finished my preparations early in the day, and decided I could take the time to begin the walnut gathering. I headed outside with two bushel-baskets, which I soon filled with the rough-husked nuts. When the baskets were full, I hauled them to the back porch and sat down wondering about the next step. I knew the nuts themselves were deep inside these tough outer skins, and that they couldn't begin to dry until the husks had been removed. I supposed the husks would eventually split open of their own accord, but I saw no reason not to speed the process along, so I walked into the kitchen for a knife.

Inside Susie asked me what I was doing, and I told her.

"Shouldn't you ask somebody? You've never done this before," Susie said.

"How hard can it be? Just remove the husks and let the nuts inside dry." It seemed elementary to me.

Back on the porch, I attacked the first husk. It was tougher than I expected, but eventually the sharp knife sliced into the skin and penetrated until it hit something hard, the nutshell, I assumed. I turned it over and hacked a similar cut into the other side, the clear juice from the meat of the husk running onto my hands. I had hoped the outer skin could now be peeled off, but it resisted my tugging and twisting. I got a screwdriver and went at the recalcitrant husk with it, digging and prying until finally, after five minutes of high-energy labor, I shucked the outer layer off and revealed the nut inside. It still had strings of the outer flesh clinging to its surface.

After a half-hour more, I had freed a second nut, but by then I realized there had to be an easier way. At this rate, the job would take me all day.

Then, in a momentary flash of brilliance, I conceived an idea. Moving to the basement, I found a piece of scrap plywood about 12-inches square. Using a nut I'd just freed from its hull as a template, I drew a circle in the middle of wood, just slightly larger than the nut. I then clamped the board into the vice, and using my saber

20

saw, cut the circle out. Going back outside with two sawhorses, I attached the board horizontally between the two with screws, forming a little "table" with a hole in the center.

Next, I placed a walnut centered in the hole. Procuring my sledgehammer from the garage, I gave the husk a mighty whack, thinking to force it through the hole and free the nut inside. After a fashion it actually worked, though it took three blows with the hammer to work the nut out of the skin, with juice flying everywhere. And on the third hit, I broke the plywood in half. Reluctantly giving up for the moment, I decided to seek advice after all. I went inside to wash up.

As I'd been working, I noticed that the juice from the husks, though running out clear, turned dark brown on my hands. Since the work was so messy, I figured on getting it all done before washing up. But now, standing at the kitchen sink, and scrubbing my hands with soap, I discovered that the stains did not wash off. Thinking I just needed something stronger, I reached under the sink for a can of cleanser, and sprinkled a generous portion onto one hand. I rubbed my palms together and worked the cleanser between my fingers. Then rinsing off, I found the unstained parts of my hands very clean — and the walnut-stained parts as dark as ever.

Not to be defeated, I got a bottle of bleach from the laundry room, poured some into a bowl, and immersed my hands in the undiluted chemical, turning my nose away from the smell. After soaking and scrubbing, I found my hands whiter than I'd ever seen them — whiter that is, except where the walnut juice had stained them. On those patches, the deep brown color remained. It was, I finally admitted, going to have to wear off.

And that's when I remembered that in less than 24 hours, those same stained hands would be handling the blessed elements of bread and wine (actually grape juice — we were Methodists after all!) and holding them out under parishioners' faces as they knelt at the Communion rail to receive them.

I went to Susie to tell her my tale of woe. As I walked in the room, Susie looked at me strangely for a second, but listened as I told her my plight.

"Well," she said, "when you get to that part of the service, you'll just have to explain what happened and that your hands really are clean."

"I guess so."

"But actually, you might want to have your story ready before that," Susie said with a grin.

"Why?"

"Because, Sweetheart," she said, standing up and kissing me on the nose, "you've got a faceful of interesting dark brown freckles!" She exited, laughing.

And so it went. The whole congregation had a good laugh at my expense, and nobody seemed to mind in the least being served Communion by a freckle-faced, stained-hand pastor.

After the service, one of the older farmers said, "You know, there is a way to get the nuts if you still want them. Just dump 'em in your gravel driveway and leave 'em there for a few days, running over them with your car as you come and go. This will remove or loosen the majority of husks. The rest will be loose enough to pry out manually, but wear gloves — and in your case," he added with a smirk, "probably face protection too. Welcome to the country."

4. Neighbors

Like many small rural townships, Thornberry had some problems because it had no zoning laws. On their own property, people could pretty much do as they pleased, and while most residents had enough pride to keep their places looking good, a few didn't put much energy into upkeep. In Thornberry, the worst appearing property belonged to Ray Sandauer. It wasn't just that the place looked rundown, and it did, but also that Ray operated his trucking business out of his home. He owned three semis, one or another of which was always broken down and sitting in his oily driveway with the motor exposed. Old truck parts littered the property and the house was desperately in need of paint and shoring up. The ramshackle outbuildings and a partially collapsed barn added to the eyesore quality of the place.

Although Mrs. Sandauer, a quiet woman who kept to herself, dressed tidily enough, Ray's appearance — even in a community where farmers routinely wore work clothes — was cause for comment. His ragged shirts and jeans were always greasy, understandable when he was working on his trucks, but he came to community functions dressed similarly. His outfits, combined with his unkempt curly beard and shoulder-length stringy hair, conspired to give him an outlaw look.

No one had had any direct problems with him, but the look of his homestead irritated his neighbors. Without zoning laws, there were limits to what they could do about it. But sometime before my arrival in Thornberry, a few of Ray's neighbors had decided to try a legal action to force him to clean up his place. The plan had failed, I was told, largely because Marti, the widow who lived immediately next door to Ray, had been unwilling to support it.

That surprised me, for Marti's property was immaculately kept, and I assumed the blot on the landscape next to her would have bothered her. But Marti had steadfastly refused to have anything to do with the complaint.

Then one Sunday, I noticed that the flowers on the altar that morning had been given by Marti in memory of her son, Ricky. I knew that Marti had a grown son; she'd often spoken about him and about her grandson, who was named Ricky. But I hadn't heard about a son by that name. When I inquired of Marti about him, she only said, "He died as a child. It was a long time ago. My grandson is named after him."

The choir director overheard my conversation, and when Marti had left, he told me the story. One day, when both of Marti's boys were small, a teenaged girl was babysitting them. While she was in another room, the boys wandered outside and began playing in the farm pond on the property. Minutes later the older boy, age 5, came running in to tell the babysitter that his brother was in the water. Running outside, the sitter saw no sign of the child in the murky water and began screaming for help.

Ray, working on a truck next door, heard her and came running. Quickly grasping what had happened, he ordered the sitter to phone the rescue squad, and then he raced into the pond, diving again and again until he found the little boy. Hauling Ricky out, he tried to revive him, using CPR, which he continued until the rescue workers arrived. Regrettably, it was all too late. Ray phoned the parents, and stood by them during the next horrible hours. And he did his best to console the horrified brother and the guilt-stricken sitter.

I understood now why Marti would never support any action against her neighbor, for that's what Ray was — her neighbor indeed.

5. Freed by the Word

"I was afraid," the old man said. It was the fourth time in three minutes that Vern had made the statement. He was old enough — 83 — to be excused for repeating himself, and he did it again.

"I know it sounds silly to you, Reverend," Vern said, "but I was afraid."

I had first seen the old man two weeks earlier sitting with Ann Mills in the Sunday worship service. Afterward, Ann introduced the visitor to me as "my Uncle Vern," and added, "He'll be staying with us from now on." Later, I learned that Vern was a bachelor. With his health beginning to fail, Ann and her family had opened their home to him.

The next Sunday Vern was in the pew with Ann again. During the preaching, he leaned forward, resting his chin on his folded hands, which were cupped over his cane. He appeared to be listening intently.

On Monday morning, Ann phoned. "Uncle Vern has something on his mind. He won't tell me what it is, but said he'd like to talk to you alone. Would it be possible for you to visit him sometime?" I agreed to come that afternoon, which was why I was now listening to the sad-faced old man talk about the fear that had blighted his teenage years and cemented him into decades of loneliness.

Vern had just told me about growing up as a member of a strict church, peopled by a stern group of "bluenoses" (Vern's word). "They were sin-chasers," Vern said. "They thought it was their job to root out sin. I was afraid of them."

He looked off into space and then back at me. "I lived in a small town. No matter where I went, there were people from the church. When I was 17, this pretty girl moved in down the street from my family. We went to the same school. One day, I noticed her walking home a little way ahead of me. We were going the same route, and I thought maybe I could catch up and walk with her.

"But then I thought, 'Suppose some of those bluenoses look out their windows and see me. What will they think?' So I turned at the next corner and went home another way."

I was fascinated, and asked, "Did you think those bluenoses, as you call them, were against normal courting between young people?"

"Yes, at the time I did."

"Had those people said things to you about such behavior before?" I asked.

"No. But I thought they would. When I was 18, I started working at the mill. I had a car. Sometimes I would see this woman from the mill office walking home. I thought of offering her a ride, but I was afraid of what those sin-chasers would say. I'd heard of some cases where men were criticized for offering rides to women."

"Didn't you ever date?" I asked.

"Once. There was this girl who worked in the store where I shopped for groceries. I kind of liked her. I finally worked up the courage to ask her to a band concert in the park one Sunday afternoon. She agreed to go, and said she'd bring a picnic lunch."

Vern shook his head. "I should have known that it wouldn't work out. Some of the church people were at the concert, and I could see them looking at us. After a while, the girl reached over and took my hand. I knew those bluenoses would not approve, and I started to sweat."

"What happened?"

"I got up and ran away. I never shopped in that store again."

Tears were running down the old man's cheeks as he added, "I stopped going to church and never went near any women after that. Just worked and kept to myself."

His words struck me with a sense of tragedy. His was an unfulfilled life. I wondered why he wanted me to know his story. I doubted that his impression of his childhood church as one filled with only joyless, judgmental people was accurate. In every age, there are those who take a legalistic approach to Christianity and reduce it to a somber list of don'ts, assuming that anything pleasurable is automatically sinful. Yet, in most Christian circles, the majority hear the gospel message as one of kingdom joy, and embrace the faith as an enriching and redeeming experience. Sadly, Vern had

apparently assumed the attitudes of the former group character-
ized the entire membership of his childhood congregation.

And even if the old man was right about the puritanical bent of
that lot, he apparently had not grown beyond it. Most people who
grow up in such environments still manage a reasonable social life
and are able to court and find a mate. Vern had obviously been
socially backward — painfully so, probably neurotically so — and
had been terrorized as much by the imagined opinions of others as
by anything they'd actually said or done to him.

"How did you feel about keeping to yourself like that?" I asked.

Vern pulled a red bandanna handkerchief from his pocket and
wiped his eyes. "Not very good. It's been a lonely life. But, you
know, being alone gives a man a lot of time to fill. I've read hun-
dreds of books since then. Last year, I decided to read the Bible. I
hadn't had anything to do with the Bible since I stopped going to
church way back then. But I finally decided that I ought to read it."

As he continued, his facial expression grew less grim. "I started
at the beginning, right at Genesis, chapter one. It was pretty tough
going for a while, but I finally finished the Old Testament.

"After I got into the Gospels, it struck me that Jesus was no
sin-chaser. There was nothing bluenose about *him*. It was a great
compliment the Pharisees paid Jesus when they criticized him for
eating with sinners!" Vern chuckled.

"In John, I read about a woman who'd been caught in adultery
by some Pharisees. I bet she was just as afraid of those Pharisees as
I was of those bluenoses. But Jesus didn't condemn her. He told
her to sin no more, but he didn't condemn her."

The man became increasingly animated as he spoke. "I wish
I'd read the Bible years ago. I've learned something from reading
about Jesus. He didn't come to make us miserable, but to save us
from destroying ourselves."

"That's very insightful," I said. "You're right."

"Anyway, that's why I wanted to talk to you," Vern said. "I'd
like to join your church." He was absolutely beaming.

"I'd be very happy to receive you into the church," I said, "but
in light of what you've told me, I think I should warn you that

while we've got a great bunch of Christian people in the congregation, you might occasionally run into one or two who are kind of like those bluenoses."

"That's okay, Reverend," the old man said with a smile. "I'm not afraid anymore."

6. Compensation

"That's my medicine," Louie said.

"I don't think so, Louie," I said, looking askance at the weathered little man at my door, dressed in dirty, mismatched clothes.

His statement was to get me to overlook the boozy aroma emanating from his entire personage and especially from his mouth, which had led me to observe, "You've been drinking."

Louie was one of my "regulars," a person who could be counted on to show up at my door at least once a month seeking material help to tide him over until his next welfare check arrived.

Our congregation, like almost every church in America, took seriously the biblical injunction to feed the hungry and clothe the naked. We had established a "Local Missions" fund in which resided about $200, and it was the duty of the pastor to administrate it, giving out vouchers that could be spent at area grocery stores and gas stations. Thus it was not uncommon to find people at my door requesting help. For the most part, these were people I'd come to know from their previous visits, though none were church members.

Louie was such a person. His family, such as it was, had been in poverty for at least three generations, and the practice of being permanently unemployed (leading to yet more need) showed no signs of abating with Louie. While I usually gave him a food voucher when he came by, I wouldn't do it when he was clearly intoxicated.

"No, it's really my medicine," Louie said again.

"Sorry. Come back when you're sober." I spoke kindly, because I felt genuine sympathy for Louie, even if his problems were of his own making.

Louie wobbled away.

Handling the Local Missions fund was a part of my work that I liked the least. In other circumstances, helping others can be uplifting, but with the "regulars," I often felt that I was perpetuating a cycle of dependency. In addition, some of those who came were rough-looking characters, who when steeped in alcohol, behaved unpredictably. I'd never been harmed, but one man had punched out the glass in my door when he didn't receive as large a food voucher as he wanted.

More than my own safety, however, I worried about Susie's. I was often out of the house, and it would fall to her to tell people to come back when I would be home, which of course, also told them she was there alone. So far, no one had been belligerent with her, but it was a concern.

In addition to those who came to our door seeking help, there were requests by telephone. Those were usually from people I didn't know. Generally these were folks who had gotten help so often from the church nearest them that they were now being turned away, and so they were prospecting to find other sources of help. Some had legitimate needs but others were "working the system," and it was always difficult for us pastors to tell one from the other.

One Friday evening when I was particularly tired and looking forward to a restful evening at home, I received such a call from a woman in another township 15 miles away. There were at least four other churches nearer to her, so I assumed that she had exhausted all of those sources of help and was now reaching out farther. But she had such a tale to tell — hungry children in her house, she said, and not able to reach anyone at any of the churches nearer to her. My internal "bogus story" meter was going off, but of course, I couldn't be sure. And since it was Friday night, the county welfare offices were closed so I couldn't call there to check her need or to see if she really had any children.

My immediate inclination was to say no, but then, *suppose her story was true*. If there really were hungry children in the house, they shouldn't suffer because of their parents' misfortune, lack of planning, bad habits, or unwillingness to work. So I finally agreed to give her a voucher to use at her local supermarket. I told her I'd have it ready for her to pick up.

But then she said she had no transportation. Could I deliver it? A 30-mile round trip mind you. I was about to say no, but I again considered that there really might be hungry children there.

I made the delivery.

30

When I drove into the woman's driveway, there were four vehicles sitting there, and no children in the house. They were all out with their father at that moment, the woman said, which of course begged the question of what *he* was using for transportation. So she was working the system — though from the look of her place, her poverty was real enough.

I left the voucher with her, but I drove away feeling as if I'd been taken for a sucker.

Jesus observed that "the poor you will always have with you," and for those of us trying to assist them, the whole matter remained unsolvable. One thing you certainly couldn't count on was getting any kind of warm feeling or sense of satisfaction when helping the poor. Some didn't even seem appreciative, and maybe they shouldn't be. It can't be easy standing on the outside and looking at the bounty others have.

But then, you never knew. Take Louie. I never heard what changed in his life — or if indeed it had changed — but the next three times he arrived at my door, he was at least sober. And then, I didn't see him for several months.

When he finally came again, I was painting the kitchen, and was thoroughly paint-splattered. Seeing Louie through the door glass, I grabbed my voucher pad. Opening the door, I immediately observed that while dressed as usual in ill-fitting and mismatched clothes, Louie's outfit was clean, and he had on a necktie. His hair was combed and his face was freshly shaved. With him was a woman of similar age, tidily dressed in hand-me-down clothes but so skinny she appeared undernourished. She was smiling.

"This here's Beverly," Louie said. "We'd like you to marry us, Reverend."

Surprised, I said, "All right. When would you like to have the ceremony?"

"Right now. We got the license and everything." He held up a packet of papers.

I looked down at my messy old clothes and the freckles of paint on my arms. "I don't look good enough for a wedding at this moment. How about at 6:00 this evening?"

"We don't care what you look like. We're all set."

31

Beverly nodded her agreement.

"Well," I said, "the day you get married is a special one. And you'll want to remember that everything was nice. How about giving me an hour to get cleaned up? We'll have the wedding in the church. I've got a camera, and I'll have my wife come and take your picture."

Louie looked thoughtful. "Yes, that would be nice. What do you think, Bev?"

"That sounds really good," Beverly answered.

So that's what we did. Cleaned up and wearing my dark suit, I performed the ceremony. Susie played the wedding march on the piano, and afterward took pictures of the smiling pair. I promised to have them developed and mailed to Louie.

"Thanks, Reverend," Louie said. "That's real nice." Then, taking his bride's hand, he led her out of the church.

So passed the awkward moment when newlywed husbands usually handed me an envelope. While I never charged for weddings, most couples gave me an honorarium of between $25 and $50. With the small church salary, such gifts were a welcome addition to our income. But when I agreed to officiate for Louie and Beverly, I knew I wouldn't be getting an honorarium.

So I wasn't even thinking about that when Louie came running back into the church. "I almost forgot this, Reverend." Louie thrust a small envelope toward me. Knowing Louie's precarious financial situation, I almost refused it, but something about his eagerness changed my mind.

"Thank you, Louie."

After he left, I opened the envelope. Inside were three one-dollar bills.

I couldn't remember ever being as well compensated.

7. Summer Rain

All in all, Thornberry was a pretty quiet place, where big news usually referred to something like a change in menu for the annual ox roast. Yet one of my first funerals was for a young man who'd been shot to death as an innocent bystander in someone else's quarrel. He had grown up in the church and was loved and respected by the congregation. At the time of his death, he was just 21 and newly married.

The tragedy of Eddie's death was compounded by irony. Years before, his mom and dad had moved their family to our quiet little farm community to escape the violence of the neighborhood in Cleveland where they'd been living. One cost of the move was Ed senior's daily drive. His job was still in the city, and each workday he drove more than 100 miles round trip to work, a sacrifice he willingly made for his family's well being.

Moving from an urban life to a rural area must have been unsettling for the family as well. Fortunately, they were warmly welcomed in our church, and by the time I was appointed there, Eddie's family was well established in the congregation.

As Eddie and his brother Randy, a year younger, reached their teenage years, they went to work for farmers in the community, helping with the summer chores and the fall harvests. They were both hard workers and much appreciated by those who employed them.

But at 20, Eddie married a young woman from the city and moved back there where steady work was easier to find. Within six months, he returned to our hamlet in a coffin.

The midsummer day of the funeral dawned bright and sunny. We held the service in the church and then traveled in procession to the cemetery. There, the casket bearing Eddie's body was placed on the lowering rig that had been set up over the gaping grave. The group of us, perhaps 60 strong, gathered around it while I spoke the traditional words of committal:

Forasmuch as it hath pleased Almighty God to call unto himself the soul of our departed brother, Edward, we tenderly commit his body to the ground in the blessed hope that as he has borne the image of the earthly, so may he also bear the image of the heavenly. Earth to earth, ashes to ashes, dust to dust.

Throughout the time at the cemetery, Randy, Eddie's brother, had been quietly weeping. But as I brought the graveside service to a close, his emotion overflowed, and he began sobbing loudly. Suddenly he jumped up and threw himself across his brother's coffin, clutching it tightly and crying, "No, no, no."

For a moment we all stood there, not quite sure what to do. Then his mother and father came to him and tried to get him to leave the casket. But Randy was lost in his grief and held on fiercely. Others of us tried to comfort the young man too, but none of us could break through.

Unnoticed during all of this, the sky had been changing. In a matter of minutes it shifted from bright blue to dark gray, and without preamble, heavy rain began pelting us, a furious summer storm. The downpour accomplished what the rest of us could not. Randy, still shaking with emotion, finally loosened his grip on the casket and allowed himself to be led to a waiting car.

I suppose some might say the sudden and unexpected rain was a fortunate coincidence. But I suspect it was Providence, a gift of mercy for a family that had lost too much.

8. The Back of the House

The attractive young lady sitting opposite me was a puzzle. On the one hand, she wore her brown hair long and flowing, a style popular among young women then. But she was dressed formally — a skirt and blouse, nylon hose, and four-inch high heels. The outfit set off her slender figure nicely, but it was too dressy since she was neither coming from nor going to work.

Deborah's attire no longer surprised me. She'd been dressed similarly when she first showed up in church four months earlier with her little girl in tow. Her elegant appearance had been appropriate in that context, though she was the only woman in heels quite that high. But every time I encountered her thereafter, even at casual events where other women showed up in slacks, shorts, or jeans, Deborah was dressed in high fashion, including the tall heels that looked terribly uncomfortable but which accentuated her shapely legs.

As a newcomer to worship, Deborah had supplied an address on a visitor card. So, according to my usual practice, I made a pastoral visit during the week following. Even there in her home, except for wearing flat shoes, Deborah was dressed up.

During the brief time I spent in her immaculate residence, I learned that she and her husband Eldon had moved into the community only three weeks earlier. Eldon was employed at a factory a few miles away and was at work then. Deborah was currently unemployed, but said she enjoyed being a homemaker and caring for their daughter Patricia. The child, age 4, was sitting at the counter in the spotless kitchen coloring. She was wearing a lacy dress with a white pinafore, anklets, and shiny patent-leather shoes.

I had stopped by unannounced. Seeing their garb, I thought I might be interrupting preparations to go somewhere. "I notice you two are dressed up. Are you getting ready to leave?" I asked.

"No, we just like looking good for Daddy, don't we, Patricia?"

"Uh-huh," the little girl responded, not looking up from her coloring.

Deborah and Patricia had continued coming to church, though never accompanied by Eldon, and even after seven months of their regular attendance, I still had not met him. During that time, Susie, who was one of the least jealous people I knew, had developed an uneasiness about Deborah. "You be careful of her," Susie had told me.

"Why? What's she done?"

"Nothing. It's just a feeling, and maybe I'm misreading her. But still, be careful."

I'd seen nothing about Deborah to alarm me, but I'd never known Susie to react to anyone like that, so I did not dismiss her words out of hand. But at the time, Susie was in the early months of pregnancy, something we were both excited about, and I wondered if the hormonal changes taking place in her had affected her judgment.

Now Deborah was in my study by appointment. She'd requested it the previous Sunday, suggesting Tuesday afternoon, when Patricia would be visiting her grandmother.

We'd been talking about nothing much for a few moments, as I waited for Deborah, who was wringing her hands, to explain the reason for the appointment.

Finally she said, "I wanted to talk to you about my husband. He's ... well ... very demanding."

She stopped, and I sensed that she was looking at me to see if she'd said enough yet for me to respond. She hadn't, of course, and I waited for her to continue.

"Well," she said. "I work hard to keep our home nice and to take good care of Patricia. That's a big job."

"I noticed how nicely kept your house was when I was there," I said.

"Thanks, but I don't think Eldon appreciates all that I do." She stopped again, as if what she'd just said explained everything.

Eventually, I prompted her. "What does he do that makes you feel that way?"

"He sometimes forgets to take his boots off right away when he comes home from work." She went silent again, casting her eyes down.

36

I waited.

"Sometimes he leaves his dirty clothes on the bedroom floor."

"That must be annoying," I said, suspecting we hadn't come to the real reason for her visit yet. "Are those the main things that bother you?"

"Well ... no. You see ... ah ... well ... he wants us to go to the back of the house a couple times a week." This last came out in a gush. She looked directly at me for a few seconds after speaking, and then suddenly looked away.

I wasn't positive I understood the meaning of going "to the back of the house," but I thought I knew. "Do you mean he wants to have sexual relations twice a week?"

At once Deborah blushed. "Yes."

"And that seems unreasonable to you?"

"Yes. I mean, we've been married five years."

"I'm not sure I see the connection."

"Well, we're not newlyweds anymore."

"There are no rules about how frequently married couples have sex. It's a matter of what's comfortable and pleasurable for the two of you."

"But we can't keep going to the back of the house now. We have our child."

"You mean Eldon wants to have sex when Patricia is awake?"

"No, it's not that ... well, you know ... I mean, we don't plan to have any more children."

"And sex is only for having children?"

Deborah didn't answer but started weeping, dabbing her eyes with a hankie she'd pulled out of her purse. Eventually she said, "No, I guess not." As she spoke, she crossed her legs, causing her skirt to ride up a good bit. When she made no move to adjust it, Susie's warning came back to me.

I said nothing, assuming Deborah would explain, but she seemed at a loss for words. Finally I tried a different tack. "Is Eldon abusive in any way?"

Deborah seemed startled and surprised. "Oh, no. Not at all. He's very gentle ... very kind."

"Tell me about him."

37

That question released a flood of words. She told me of their first meeting on a blind date arranged by a mutual friend. Deborah had just been dropped by her previous boyfriend, and Eldon, though not much of a talker, had been comforting and friendly. After a few dates, he had suggested marriage. "He seemed so nice," Deborah said, "so I said, 'Yes.' "

Patricia had been born 10 months later. Eldon proved to be a good provider and an easy-going man. Deborah never said so in so many words, but I soon gathered that she felt she had married beneath her strata, both intellectually and socially. She again mentioned his pressure on her "to go to the back of the house" every few days.

From time to time, as Deborah spoke, she cast little glances my way that conflicted with the words she was speaking. Although not very overt, she was behaving seductively. While her words were saying she was very reluctant about sex, her manner was saying the opposite. I wondered if she sent such mixed messages to her husband, and I began to feel sorry for the man.

Despite the things Deborah had said so far, she still had not stated directly what she wanted from me as a counselor. After several more minutes of talk that yielded little new information, I said, "Why don't you ask Eldon if he'd come in with you? We could talk together about your relationship."

"Oh, I couldn't do that," she said quickly, again giving me a bedroom-eyes look.

"It's difficult to work on your marriage without including your mate in the discussion at some point."

"He wouldn't understand."

"Still, I think you should ask him. And if you prefer, I can suggest a counseling center that specializes in marriage counseling."

Deborah looked distinctly uncomfortable. "Well, I'll think about it," she said weakly. She sat there without moving.

Moments later, I brought the session to a close, but told her she could phone me if she wanted to bring Eldon for a conversation.

As she prepared to leave, she thanked me for my time. Despite the brave smile on her face as she exited, I sensed nothing had been resolved. I wasn't sure if I had helped her at all. She'd indicated the problem was with her husband, but I suspected that a big chunk of it was with her. I'd had a couple of pastoral counseling courses in seminary, but they didn't provide enough training to delve deeply into people's psyches.

Deborah and Patricia were in church as usual the following Sunday, but not the next Sunday or the one after that, so that week, while out making home visits, I decided to stop by their house.

As I approached the front door, I heard a hammering sound deep in the house. It stopped when I rang the doorbell. A moment later, a young man, dressed in jeans and a flannel shirt, opened the door. "Hello?" he said.

I introduced myself and asked, "Are you Eldon?"

"Yes."

I explained that I'd noticed his wife and daughter's absence from church and had stopped to see if anything was wrong.

Eldon looked sad. "I guess you could say everything is wrong ... Look, I was about to have some coffee. Would you like some?"

"Sure."

"C'mon in," he said, stepping back to let me enter. Eldon was a pleasant-looking man, although I doubted most women would call him handsome.

Inside, I immediately saw that the house was in disarray. Boxes sat everywhere, some sealed and others partially packed. Eldon poured coffee into two mugs and set them on the kitchen table. "I've got sugar but the milk has gone bad."

"Black's fine."

Eldon dropped into a chair. I sat down across the table from him.

"Debbie and Patricia really liked your church," Eldon said. "I've never been one for church myself, but she said you had some good sermons."

"Thanks." I had not heard her called "Debbie" before.

"I guess you noticed the boxes."

"Yes. Are you moving?"

Eldon looked gloomy. "Debbie's taken Patricia and left me. They moved out a week ago."

"I'm sorry to hear that."

39

"She said it wasn't working out and that I was holding her back. But I don't understand. We seldom fought, and I'd always encouraged her to go to school or pursue a career or do whatever she wanted. I thought we were pretty happy. We're not rich, but we've had enough to get along comfortably." He looked down at his coffee, shaking his head.

"Is there any hope for getting back together?"

"Debbie says not. She was pretty firm when she left. That's why I'm getting the house ready to sell. There's no future here anymore."

"That must be heartbreaking."

"Yeah ... I sure wasn't expecting this. I knew things weren't perfect but I thought they were pretty good."

We talked on for several more minutes, and mostly Eldon aired his disappointment and sadness. Finally, as I stood to go, I noticed a hammer lying on the counter. I asked, offhandedly, "Do you have a lot of repairs to make?"

"No, just one room to finish up. Here, let me show you." Eldon indicated that I should follow him. He headed through a doorway. We entered a large bedroom with two massive picture windows facing the woods behind the house. The room, which was wallpapered in shades of green, was very attractive, but not quite finished. Some of the wooden trim around the windows was still to be installed. The trim, along with a saw and a box of nails lay on the floor.

"It looks like you've done a lot of work here. It's beautiful."

"Thanks, but it was all for Debbie. When we moved in here the master bedroom was just a small, dark room. Debbie wanted me to enlarge it, add the big windows and fix it up. She said she wanted a nice place for us to uh, you know ... make love. She was always dragging me back here."

"She was?" I asked, trying not to let my surprise show.

"Yeah. I mean, I'm a normal guy and all, but Debbie, she was something else. Whew! Anyway, she kept pushing for me to improve this room, and I was working hard on it. That's why I was so surprised when she left — just as I had the room nearly done."

"Yes. I guess that would confuse me too."

40

Touching the wall, Eldon said, "I had just hung the wallpaper she'd picked out. She moved out two days later."

Walking back to the kitchen, Eldon added, "I guess someone else will get to enjoy the Green Room now."

"The 'Green Room.' Good name for it."

"Yeah, but Debbie never called it that. To her, it was always 'the back of the house.'"

9. Cow 27

"I really could use the help, Reverend," Wesley said, "and with your baby coming and all, you could probably use a few extra bucks."

Wesley, one of the dairy farmers in the congregation was planning a tiling job and was short on manual laborers. He'd asked me if I could help.

"Sure," I said. "It sounds interesting."

"Good. Be there at 7:00 Saturday morning. I'll have the milking done by then, and we'll get started."

While there is some rise and fall to the land in northeast Ohio, much of the ground is relatively flat, and often with a clay base. When it rains, water lies on ground that doesn't have good natural drainage. For farmers, this is a problem, for although crops need moisture to thrive, water that remains standing on fields too long drowns out the crops. Tiling, a procedure to improve drainage, is the solution.

To tile a field, special machinery is used to dig several parallel trenches about four feet deep across a field, with the floor of the trenches sloping slightly toward where natural drainage can take over. A piping system with openings every foot or two to receive water is installed in the trenches, and then covered with straw. Finally the dirt is pushed back in to refill the trenches. When rainwater seeps into the earth, it eventually makes its way to these piping systems where it trickles in through the openings and flows away.

Today, the piping used is continuous flexible plastic tubing, with numerous holes in the tubing walls to let water in. But in the early years of my ministry, the plastic tubing had not yet been introduced. The system commonly used then consisted of baked clay cylinders called tiles, each about 18 inches long and 6 inches in diameter. There were no holes in them, but the tiles were laid in the trench leaving about a quarter-inch gap between each one for water to enter.

Since tiling fields was such a big job and required unique machinery, most farmers hired tiling contractors to install it in their field. Wesley, like most other farmers in Thornberry, had done that. But now Wesley had decided that the lane leading from his barn to the pasture should be tiled as well. When it rained, the lane turned so muddy that he had to hose down his cows when they came in the barn to be milked. And since the lane, though long, was narrow enough to require only one trench, Wesley had rented a trenching machine and resolved to do the work himself, assisted by his teen-age son and now, his unwary pastor.

Come Saturday morning, I arrived as agreed at 7:00. Wesley and his son, Peter, were already in the lane, tinkering with the machine. Several palletes of tiles were stationed at intervals down the lane. I walked to where the father and son stood, and after greeting me, Wesley handed me a pair of work gloves. "Here. You'd better wear these. Those tiles are rough."

We began at once. The trenching machine consisted of a tractor-like body with a huge digging wheel attached to its side. The device, with Wesley at the controls, began crawling down the center of the lane, slowly chiseling a trench and dumping the dirt on the opposite side from the machine. Peter and I labored in its wake placing the tiles end to end in a straight line in the bottom of the ditch. Peter worked in the ditch itself while I shuttled back and forth between the pallets and the trench, hauling the tiles, two at a time, to him. After the first hour, we traded places, and continued in that fashion throughout the morning.

Of course, it wasn't quite that simple. Periodically, the digging wheel stalled on buried rocks too big for it to handle, and then all three of us worked with shovels and spud bars until we had extracted the obstruction. The sun rose, and the whole process was hot, sweaty work.

Wesley was right about the tiles being rough, for by mid-morning, the tough cloth gloves Peter and I wore were shredding, and Wesley issued us each a new pair.

By noon, we were slightly over halfway down the lane, and Wesley called a halt for lunch. The father and son were used to long days in the fields, and were still going strong. I, however, had been dragging for the last hour and was grateful for the break.

"Shouldn't I get the front-end loader and push the dirt back over the part we've finished?" Peter asked his father, referring to their tractor with a scoop mounted on the front. "It would protect what we've done."

"No," Wesley said. "We'll do that later."

Peter wasn't convinced. "I think we should close it up now. Come on, Dad. I can do it pretty quick."

But Wesley wasn't having any of it. "It'll keep." He led the way toward the house where his wife had a huge farm lunch waiting.

After we'd eaten, the three of us resumed our task, toiling through the hot afternoon. By 3:30, the entire trench lay open, and Peter and I placed the final tiles.

It would soon be time for the afternoon milking, and Peter headed for the pasture, carefully closing the gate so the cows coming in couldn't use the lane. He was going to drive them into the barn by another route. Wesley maneuvered the trenching machine toward the barn and I followed on foot.

As Wesley parked the machine outside the barn, we heard some bellowing from within. "One of the heifers must be in heat," Wesley said. Heifers were the young female cows that had not yet been bred. Having had no offspring, they were not producing milk. Thus, for the economy of the farm, it was important that heifers be bred when they came into heat. In fact, it was an opportunity not to be missed, for at other times, they would not welcome the bull. So important was it, that heifers were not turned out to the pasture with the lactating cows, but remained in the barn so they would be noticed when they were ready.

Although Wesley's herd included nearly 100 cows yielding milk, and a couple dozen heifers, there was only one bull. Most male offspring, once they were old enough, were sold off to slaughterhouses for meat. Only an occasional bull calf was raised to maturity to service the cows, and those were usually swapped between farmers to prevent inbreeding.

To farmers like Wesley, cows were primarily milk factories. Though he treated them well, they were hardly pets. When they were no longer able to bear calves and produce milk, they were sold for hamburger. Thus, none of the cows had names. Instead, each animal had a metal tag in her right ear stamped with a number. The bull, however, had no number. In his distinctive role with the herd, he'd received a name. He was Elmer, a massive animal that occupied the first stall in the barn. A stanchion — a loose-fitting steel framework attached to the stall — surrounded his massive neck and kept him from moving around much. Every stall had a stanchion, and when the cows came in for their twice-daily milkings, they obediently put their head through the stanchions to reach the feed on the other side. Peter or Wesley then moved down the line snapping the stanchions shut. The heifers, however, roamed loose in a pen.

Wesley asked me if I would like to watch the procedure, and when I said yes, we stepped into the barn, leaving the door open. Inside, there was a sense of suppressed activity, with the normally docile animals lowing and milling about. The heifer in heat, wearing an ear tag with the number 27 on it, was moving in the pen, and Elmer, evidently catching her scent, was tugging against his stanchion.

Wesley, with a halter in hand, opened the pen and pushed his way through the young animals to cow 27. Clamping his arm around the young animal's neck, he slipped the halter on her head and then attached a lead rope to it. Tugging the rope, he led the prancing heifer out of the pen and into an empty stall, where, in her excited state, she resisted extending her head through the stanchion. After a couple of tries to get her to cooperate, Wesley merely tied the lead rope to the stanchion.

Leaving cow 27, Wesley then walked to Elmer's stall. Clipping a lead rope to the huge bull's halter, he opened the stanchion and led Elmer, who moved quite eagerly toward the young cow.

Within seconds, Elmer reared up and mounted the young cow, who was now fairly dancing in the stall. Completing the act, Elmer returned to all fours, and then, with a sudden movement, reared up again and repeated the action. The bull, apparently satisfied, now stood quietly, and Wesley took him back to his stall.

Cow 27, however, moved wildly, tugging at her rope with jerking motions of her head and bucking. Wesley, returning to her, said, "I guess I should have gotten her into the stanchion. Heifers can get pretty excited when they're being bred." Just then, 27 lunged backward hard, snapping her lead rope. Without an instance's hesitation, she bolted out the open barn door and ran down the lane. Wesley took off in hot pursuit.

27 showed no signs of slowing, and when Wesley yelled at her, she leaped sideways, landing in the open trench. I could hear tiles smashing under her hooves.

He said some more things too that I didn't hear, for by now 27 was loping down the trench with Wesley running behind, moving out of earshot. Sprinting behind, I could see Wesley's fist upraised.

At that moment, Peter, returning from the field, spotted the running cow and climbed over the gate at the far end of the lane to head her off. Seeing him, the excited beast, by now near the end of the trench, suddenly halted. Wesley was beside her in a second, grabbing her halter. Peter took the other side, and with father and son tugging, the animal climbed out of the trench. As I caught up, I could hear Wesley saying, "You goddam cow! You mangy, goddam bastard!" Then, seeing me, he suddenly looked embarrassed.

Cow 27 stood still now, sides heaving, and Wesley told Peter to take her back to the barn. Then he and I began walking back as well, surveying the damage to our day's work.

It was significant. Nearly every fourth or fifth tile was broken and in places, the cow's passage had caused dirt from the sides of the trench to fall in. It would have to be cleaned out by hand as the tiles were replaced.

Surprisingly, however, Wesley seemed more concerned at that moment about his outburst. "I guess I kind of lost my temper," he said to me sheepishly. "That's not a very good way to behave in front of my minister, now is it? I'm sorry."

"It looks like you had pretty good reason," I said.

"I suppose, but it feels like being caught with my pants down."

"I'm granting you absolution," I said, grinning, and jokingly made the sign of the cross with my hand, something not normally done in our denomination.

Wesley went suddenly quiet.

I worked quite often for Wesley after that, helping with milking and harvesting, and never heard him curse again. Peter later commented on it. "Dad's never been really profane, but it used to slip out when things went really wrong. Not anymore though. He told me that a man has to take absolution seriously and mend his ways."

10. Into Every Life

Frank put me in a bind. After he brought his wife Christine home from the hospital that autumn day, he told me the prognosis. "It's terminal," he said. "They removed the tumor, but the cancer has spread. She's going to have chemotherapy to buy her some time, but she probably hasn't got more than a year."

"I'm so sorry," I said. "How is she taking the news?"

"We haven't told her. I think it's better for her not to know. So I have to ask you not to mention it either. I don't think she could take it."

"Are you sure, Frank? Often it's better that people know so that they have time to make their peace with things and say their goodbyes."

"Not in this case. I know Christine. With no hope, she'd just give up."

I knew Christine too. I'd been her pastor for more than four years. While I couldn't claim the years of acquaintance with her that Frank had, I suspected he failed to recognize the depth of stability in his wife. In her committee work at the church, I'd seen a rocklike steadiness in her.

But this was not the moment to tell a grieving man he might be misjudging his own wife. "All right, Frank. I won't bring it up ... How are *you* doing?"

"Awful. I don't know how I'll get along without her. But I can't be down in front of her. I've got to keep her spirits up."

I doubted that was the healthiest approach for either of them, but I saw that Frank wasn't ready to deal with his emotions yet, so I said only, "I'll pray for both of you."

"Thanks. Let me take you in to see her." After bringing Christine home from the hospital, he'd installed her on a rented hospital bed in their dining room. Their bedroom was on the second floor of the old farmhouse, but Christine was too weak to climb stairs. He'd placed the bed next to the dining room's large picture window, so Christine had a view of the farm she loved. "Preacher's come to see you, Dear," he said buoyantly as he led me into the room.

49

Christine, looking desperately pale and a lot older than her 46 years, smiled wanly from the bed. "Hello, Reverend Payton. It's nice of you to stop by."

"Not at all. I'm glad to see you home."

Frank pulled up a chair for me near the bed. "Have a seat, Reverend. I'll leave you two to talk for a while. Got some things to do in the barn." He made his exit.

"Poor Frank," Christine said. "This has all been so hard on him."

"It's pretty rough on both of you. You've been through a lot."

"Ah, well, into every life ..."

We talked on, and I assiduously avoided the forbidden topic. Eventually I inquired about their married daughter, Megan, and the child she was expecting in four months, which would be Frank and Christine's first grandchild.

"At least I should last long enough to see the baby," Christine said.

My face must have revealed something, for Christine added, "Frank said I didn't know, didn't he?"

"Uh ... yes. Yes, he did."

"*He* doesn't think I do. *He* certainly didn't tell me. But he was being way too evasive when I asked him what the doctor said, so I asked the doctor myself later. He said Frank had told him not to tell me, but since I asked, he thought I should know the truth."

"How *do* you feel about it, Christine?"

"Well, it knocked the wind out of me for a bit, but since I don't have a choice, I guess I'll get used to it. Actually, it's Frank I'm worried about. He's a wonderful man, but he's never been very good at expressing his feelings."

"Have you considered just telling him that you know?"

"I don't think he's ready to handle it. It would just make it harder on him right now. But maybe later."

"I think it is important, Christine. At some point, you'll both need to open up with each other. I think together you'll carry this thing better than you possibly can separately."

"You're probably right. But not today. Please don't tell him that I know."

"Of course I won't," I said. We talked a little longer, and then I prayed with Christine and left.

The surgery itself did bring Christine some improvement in the short term, and she stood the subsequent chemotherapy better than expected. None of that changed her overall prognosis, but at least she had a few months where she was able to be out of bed and live a somewhat normal life. She made it to church for the Christmas services and by the time the grandchild, a baby girl, was born in January, Christine was able to help her daughter care for the newborn. And a few weeks later, she was present in church — wearing a wig to cover the hair loss from the chemo — when I baptized the baby in front of the congregation.

Although we all knew the child's name, the baptism ritual specifies that after the pastor has taken the baby into his arms, he asks the child's name. So, holding the tiny girl close to my pastoral robes, I asked, "What name is given this child?"

"Christine Elizabeth," said Megan, holding her husband's hand.

I glanced over to where Christine was sitting with Frank, and noted that she was beaming.

Christine came to church again the next Sunday, but two days later, she became so weak she had to be taken to the hospital where she remained for a couple of days while receiving a transfusion. This reinvigorated her enough to return home, but no longer did she venture outside, for church or any other purpose. She spent most of her time in the rented bed sleeping or looking out the large window. Megan brought the baby over every few days, friends stopped by, and I made it a point to visit Christine frequently. To each visitor, Frank mentioned that "She doesn't know," and asked the visitor not to discuss Christine's terminal diagnosis with her. As he led me to her bedside, Christine, turning her gaze from the window, said, "Look, Frank, the buds are showing on the maple tree. Spring's coming early this year. I miss being outside."

"Don't worry, Dear," Frank responded brightly, "after you get through this rough stretch, you'll be able to go out all you want. Certainly by summer."

"Sure, Frank," Christine said.

After Frank had excused himself, I sat down near the bed and began talking quietly with the drawn-looking woman. On a previous visit we had discussed her spiritual readiness for the approaching end of her life, and as I'd expected, Christine was holding onto the confidence of her faith and, in humility, to a life well lived.

So now, we talked mainly about how she was feeling. Then she asked, "Is Frank still giving the 'She-doesn't-know' speech?"

"Yes."

"Bless him. He's a fine man. And he's taking really good care of me."

"That's wonderful."

"Yes. But it's wearing him out, what with keeping the farm going and everything."

"I'm sure it's important to him to be here when you need him, though."

"Yes, and I love him all the more for it."

Christine went quiet for moment, and then she said, "I don't think it's going to be much longer now."

"Christine," I said, "it's probably time to tell Frank, don't you think? So you can say what you want to say to each other freely while you still can. Would you like me to tell Frank that you know?"

"Oh, I don't think so. I don't want to burden him with that just now. I'll tell him myself when I think he's ready."

Afterward, I had a similar conversation with Frank. "Doctor says she hasn't got much longer," Frank said, wiping his eyes with a large bandana.

"Yes, she looks very weak. Maybe it's time to tell her the whole story so you can talk about it openly."

"Yeah, I guess I should, but I hate to crush her hope."

"I think Christine's stronger emotionally than you're giving her credit for."

"Do you? I'll give it some thought. Maybe I'll tell her tomorrow."

Christine died on the Tuesday after Easter. We had the funeral on Friday. The sky was bright blue and the air pleasantly warm as we drove in procession to the cemetery. After the graveside committal, mourners lingered in the sunshine. Frank came up and thanked me for the service. "I've had a wonderful life with Christine," he said. "I have a lot to be thankful for."

After he moved away, Megan, carrying the baby, came over and thanked me as well. I knew that Megan was in on both secrets, just as I had been, so I asked if her parents had ever shared that final bit of sad news.

"No, they never did," Megan said. "Mom was really bad Monday night and we didn't think she'd make it to morning. Dad sat by her bed all night, holding her hand. He told her several times how much he loved her and she said the same to him. But the last thing he told her was how he was looking forward to her helping him put in the garden in a few weeks."

"What'd she say to that?"

"Sure, Frank. I'm looking forward to it."

Frank never remarried, but he went on with the farm, fulfilling his roles as father and grandfather. He continued to be an active church member, and, as far as I could tell, handled his grief about as well as anyone does.

Everything I'd read and been taught in my pastoral care classes in seminary said it was a mistake for marriage partners not to confront the end of life for one together. According to the prevailing view, Frank should have at least had some regret that "they'd never said goodbye." But he didn't seem to. Somehow in his love for Christine, he'd seen it as an act of love to maintain the pretense that she was going to recover. And Christine, in the wisdom of her love for Frank, somehow knew that it was important to let him believe he was keeping up her hope.

Real life, I was finding out, didn't always conform to the definitions of my textbooks.

11. The Organ

A church crisis can be precipitated by seemingly innocent events. The Great Organ Controversy, as we came to call it, began in just such a way, with, of all things, a wedding.

Weddings are generally pretty happy affairs, and Bonnie Flint's was no exception. The ceremony, the reception afterward, the beaming bride and groom — everything about the day was splendid. Even her increasingly senile grandfather, old Harry Huffman, did nothing to blemish the event.

The tethers on Harry's mind were slipping as he aged. Now nearly 90, it wasn't uncommon for him to suddenly blurt something out loud, even in the midst of a worship service. He'd been known to shout without warning things like, "Hey, who are you?" or "Is it time for dinner yet?" The most memorable of those occasions was during a sermon a few weeks before the wedding. I'd been talking about an Old Testament passage where a bull was to be slaughtered for a sacrifice when Harry had suddenly yelled, "The cows won't like it!" The congregation had a good laugh. Perhaps a larger church wouldn't have tolerated such outbursts, but in Thornberry, where several people were related to the old man, and those who weren't remembered with respect the generous and kind old man he'd been when in his right mind, nobody really objected.

Harry lived with his son, who brought him to church and always sat with him. The son said that Harry began every day by asking, "Do we go to church today?" so it seemed important to the son that Harry come as long as he was able. What the old man actually got out of the service, of course, was anybody's guess.

But at Bonnie's wedding, he'd been blessedly silent and the day had gone smoothly for Bonnie and her new husband.

Bonnie had grown up in the Thornberry congregation and was a faithful church member. She'd even continued to attend after her mother died three years earlier, when Bonnie was 19. Bonnie had always come to church with her mother. Her father, Daniel, although a member, hadn't been to worship in years.

So maybe that was why, when Bonnie told him she'd like to be married in the church, Daniel went overboard on the arrangements — to sort of make up for letting his daughter come to church all by herself those last years.

Anyway, that's when Daniel asked the church board to let him rent an organ for the sanctuary. The church once owned an organ, but it had developed expensive problems years before. Ellie, our organist, had started using the piano to accompany the singing. At first, Ellie had missed the organ, but everyone said the piano sounded just fine. They'd eventually hauled the old organ to the dump and after a little while, no one thought any more about it.

Now Daniel Flint decided that the piano would not suffice for his daughter's wedding, even though many brides had walked down the church's aisle to its chords in the years since the organ had been discarded. Bonnie said she didn't mind the piano at all. In fact, she really wanted a simple ceremony, but Daniel wouldn't hear of it.

He asked the church's administrative board for permission to bring a rented organ in for the ceremony. No one saw a problem with that, so the board members agreed. Since the store didn't rent organs by the day, Daniel had to pay a month's rent on it. But the music store proprietor, possibly sensing a sales opportunity, suggested that the church keep the organ the full month.

Ellie was delighted. She played the Saturday wedding, and then all four of the month's Sunday services, on the new instrument. The congregation was thrilled by the sound of the organ, and by the fourth Sunday, some wondered how we'd gotten by so long without one.

On Monday morning of the week the organ was to be returned, the storeowner phoned Alan Fetman, the board chairperson, and offered to let the church keep it, for $3395. "It usually sells for $3850," he'd told Alan, "but since it's for a church, I'm able to offer you a deal. And the rent that Mr. Flint has already paid can be deducted from the price too."

Alan was impressed. He called a special session of the board to discuss the matter.

"I move we buy it," Arthur Kagel said. Arthur was a relative newcomer to the community. He'd been there "only" 11 years.

"I second the motion," Ellie said.

"Whoa. Just a minute." It was Ralph Barnes, the church treasurer. "That's a lot of money. How are you going to pay for it?"

Arthur said, "I'm sure if we put it before the congregation we can raise it quickly enough. Everybody really likes the way the organ sounds."

Several others spoke up in agreement.

"In fact," continued Arthur, "I'll pledge $100 toward the purchase myself, right now."

"So will I," another said. Others indicated that they too would gladly contribute.

"I bet we'll have the whole amount raised within two weeks!" Arthur was beginning to get excited.

But Ralph wasn't convinced. "I think we're missing something here. You all know how tight the church budget has been. Right now, we're a few thousand dollars behind in our pledge to the denominational mission fund. Arthur, if you're willing to give $100 dollars, why not give it to that?"

Arthur answered, "I'll give money to the organ fund because I can see the organ and know how my money is being used. I'm not going to send it somewhere where half of it will be used to pay some church executive's salary."

I was stunned by Arthur's attitude, but before he could respond, Hazel Williams, a widow in her late sixties, spoke up. "That's not true, Arthur. In last month's women's group magazine there was an article telling how the mission money is used. Only a tiny fraction goes to pay administrative expenses."

"Yes," said Ralph, the treasurer. "I've read some things about that too. Those funds go to help a lot of people in a lot of places around the world, and some right here in our own state."

"Maybe so," replied Arthur, "but it's not the same as hearing that organ week after week."

Melvin Calvert, Ellie's husband, hadn't said anything throughout the entire discussion, although he had listened carefully. "It seems to me," he began, "that we're letting this organ business get out of proportion." One of the older members, Melvin had attended that church his entire life. Because he had given so much of himself to the work of the congregation, and had been proven a man of friendly wisdom, folks usually listened respectfully when he spoke. "We worshiped just fine for years with the piano."

Ellie shot a look of dismay at Melvin, but if he noticed it, he did not respond. He continued: "I like the organ too, and I certainly enjoy hearing Ellie play it. But we've made a commitment to our mission fund. I think we should honor it. If we can do that and still get the organ, fine. But if we can't, then I wouldn't feel right about buying it."

"This is getting us nowhere," Arthur said impatiently. "Alan, I call for the question. You've got a motion on the floor. Let's vote."

When it came right down to it, just over half of those present voted "Yes," but it was enough to carry the motion. Ralph Barnes, Hazel Williams, Melvin Calvert, and I were among the "No's." Ellie, after hearing her husband's speech, abstained from voting at all.

After the vote Ralph said, "That's not exactly a mandate, but I guess we'll have to live with it. It kind of bothers me, though, that this whole fuss was started by a man who doesn't even come to church. Daniel Flint didn't do us any favor bringing that organ in."

As it turned out, Arthur had not been optimistic enough. The congregation raised the entire purchase price of the organ in just five days, although several families, siding with the pay-the-mission-fund faction, contributed nothing.

Thus, the next Sunday, when Ellie began the worship prelude on the organ, there was a feeling of uneasiness in the pews. We proceeded through the service, but there was a palpable air of discord souring our normally joyful worship.

After the service, I noticed Melvin talking intently to Arthur, but I didn't find out until the next Sunday what it was about. When I arrived for the service, I found a quilt draped over the organ, and Ellie, ready to begin, seated at the piano.

Melvin and Arthur stood waiting for me, and asked for permission to address the congregation before the service began.

Moving to the front of the sanctuary, Arthur spoke first. "As most of you know, I pushed the purchase of our new organ, and while I still think it was a good idea, I realize not everyone agrees. Melvin has convinced me that we may have gotten our priorities a bit mixed up, so here's what I'd like to propose. We have the organ covered up, and I suggest we leave it that way until we pay our mission commitments. Melvin's reminded me that the church is about more than what we do for ourselves. What do you think?"

This last was addressed to the congregation, but no one responded. Maybe Arthur's earlier persuasiveness about purchasing the organ had left members who'd sided with him unprepared for his change of heart. And I knew that those who had opposed him weren't anxious to reopen the controversy. In any case, the silence stretched on.

"BANG THAT KEYBOARD, SISTER!" Old Harry's bellowed words suddenly sliced through the edgy silence. From his seat in a rear pew, he continued in a shout, "LET'S TICKLE THOSE IVORIES, HONEY! WHAT ARE YOU WAITING FOR?"

That uncorked the stalemate and joyful laugher erupted from every worshiper.

"Amen!" someone shouted from the pews, and at that, Ellie struck the opening chords of her prepared prelude on the piano.

Two weeks later, enough donations had come in to catch us up on our mission fund. We officially dedicated the organ and began using it in the services.

Harry continued coming to worship, but after that morning of the organ crisis, he never again spoke out in church. He died quietly in his sleep about a year later.

According to the New Testament, the first-century church was sometimes blessed with people, who, overcome with the Holy Spirit, spoke of God in foreign languages they couldn't possibly know or praised God in unintelligible sounds that comprised a unique vocabulary of praise. New Testament scholars sometimes call these verbalizations "ecstatic utterances," but many argue that they were not intended to be an ongoing experience in the life of the church.

At Thornberry, that Sunday morning, we knew differently.

12. Night Trek

Methodist pastors change pulpits at the will of the bishop, so when the call came from my district superintendent that the bishop wanted to move me to the North Doncaster church, my staying at Thornberry was not an option. The new appointment would mean a larger parish and a salary increase, so it had to be considered a promotion. But after five years at Thornberry, I was attached to the people there and wasn't anxious to leave. Aside from a summer internship as a pastoral assistant while in college, Thornberry had been my first church appointment.

That internship had been served in a church of the denomination of my youth, one far more doctrinally conservative than the mainstream Methodists, and while there, I'd undergone a theological and career crisis that eventually resulted in my leaving that denomination, changing colleges, and throwing my lot in with the Methodists. But the summer there had cemented my decision to remain in the ministry.

I recalled the night that summer it had all come to a head. There I was, slowly plodding eastward up a hill in the darkness, shivering from the steady, clothes-soaking drizzle. I had resigned myself that the steel-laden semis laboring up the steep grade were not going to pick up a hitchhiker. Nonetheless, I resolutely stuck out my thumb each time a car or smaller truck approached. So far, however, all that had happened was that each passing vehicle just added another layer of dirty wet spray to my clothes, which made me feel the chill of the last August night all the more.

At 19, I was a bit old to be running away — and though I tried to convince myself that I was really only trying to find myself, inside I still felt like a deserter.

I thought about the little church in Steubenville, Ohio, I was running from, the church where I'd been serving a summer internship following my first year in the ministry preparation course at Royalton Bible College. For 10 weeks I had assisted the pastor: visiting the sick, conducting youth meetings, leading the children's division of the Sunday school, and directing vacation Bible school.

After two more weeks, I was to return to Royalton for the next academic year.

Would the people at the Steubenville church, people who had made me feel welcome and had given me their trust understand now? I shook myself as if to throw off the question. I couldn't afford to think about that now.

Another truck passed and I turned my head away to protect my eyes from the muddy spray churned up by the big tires. My teeth were beginning to chatter, and my arm was beginning to ache from the pull of the small suitcase I carried.

At least it had been warm in the sergeant's car. The sergeant had given me the only ride I had had so far that night. The soldier served in the Army Reserve. He was a weekend warrior on his way home when he noticed me standing by the road on the outskirts of Steubenville. After some initial small talk, we rode in silence until the sergeant asked, "Do you know where a guy can get laid around here this time of night?"

"Un-uh, no. I don't know." I was embarrassed. How would *I* know *that* kind of information? I noticed the soldier's wedding band and felt disgusted. *How*, I wondered, *would such a question be received at Royalton, where dances and handholding were taboo, dating was permitted only with prior permission from the dean, and coeducational swimming was not allowed.* In fact, the school pool had been donated by a prominent alumnus on the condition that the day a male and female were found in the pool at the same time, the pool was to be filled in with cement. The holy life.

The sergeant dropped me off on the east side of Weirton, West Virginia, where he turned north. My plans were to continue east; I was headed for a friend's house in eastern Pennsylvania. After that, I didn't know.

There had been no further rides, and I began to wonder if I would end up walking the rest of the night. Another car approached, and in the illumination of the headlights of the truck behind the car, I could make out the outlines of a man driving the car and a woman resting her head on the man's shoulder. John and Carol came to mind.

Could it really be only two weeks ago that I'd met them? Was that where this night had really begun?

Carol had grown up in the Steubenville congregation, and had spent most of this summer working at a church camp. She had met John there and they had fallen in love.

She had brought John home to meet her parents, and he was now staying with her family until the end of summer. Although John, too, had grown up under the church's influence, it did not consume his life as it had mine. John had no intentions of going into the ministry. In fact, he had worked at camp that summer to raise money for his last year of college, where he was working toward his B.A. John wanted to be a writer, and already had a few articles published. His freedom and open future drew me like a magnet. Unfortunately, they also made me feel guilty, for John's freedom represented all that I had surrendered when I entered the path I believed had been chosen for me.

Carol was another problem. She was warm, friendly, flirtatious, and very pretty. She obviously adored John, and I had no illusions that she wanted anyone but John, but she was the "type" I was attracted to, and I couldn't imagine her being married to a minister.

As the summer drew to a close, I found myself just going through the motions as I carried out my assigned responsibilities. Going back to school now seemed out of the question, but neither did I feel that I could go home; my parents and pastor had been so pleased with my career choice. *They* were so sure I was doing the right thing.

I didn't know how to tell the people in the Steubenville church that I was leaving. Everybody in the church, including the pastor and his family, had been good to me. I felt that many of the young people looked up to me. The whole congregation had heard my testimony, given in the early summer while still in the flush of enthusiasm over being sent to the church. I could not expect them to understand now. I was afraid that my flight would seem to be a faith collapse — maybe it was — and would weaken somebody else's commitment. If that happened, I did not care to be there to see it.

In the end, I didn't tell anybody; I left in the middle of the night.

West Virginia is not very wide where I was. It is a narrow strip of land, wedged awkwardly like a thumb between the borders of Ohio and Pennsylvania. Just as I approached the "Welcome to Pennsylvania" sign, a small fruit truck stopped. I climbed into the cab, glad to get out of the rain. The driver appeared young, maybe 25. I wondered what I would be doing at that age. Driving a fruit truck? There had been a boy in my class in high school who wanted to drive truck. He had been a hard kid to like, always talking about gear ratios and tandem rigs.

The cab was warm and I dozed off. It was still dark when the driver, who had introduced himself as Ed, mentioned breakfast and pulled into an all-night truck stop. He said, "If you let the waitress think you're a driver, you'll get a discount on your meal."

"Oh."

I ordered one egg, toast, and coffee. Tom had pancakes, sausage, orange juice, and coffee, and then finished the toast I left on the side of my plate.

Ed paid his bill first. From the way the cashier greeted Ed, it was obvious that she knew him. When I handed her my bill, she asked, "Are you a driver?"

"Well, uh ..."

Ed interrupted. "Yeah. He's new, just learning the route." I got the discount.

Dawn was beginning to break as we walked back to the truck. The rain had stopped. Ed jumped into the cab. I hesitated.

"Hurry up. Got to get to Pittsburgh early."

"Uh ... listen. Thanks for the ride, but you go ahead." I took my suitcase. Ed looked surprised, then shrugged his shoulders and drove away. I stood there watching the truck disappear into the sunrise. When I could see it no more, I walked back into the restaurant and laid two quarters on the cash register.

Outside again, I crossed the road. A car was coming.

I pointed my thumb west.

13. Endwork

"Good grief!" Susie said. "It's Alfred Plunket!"

"What?" I exclaimed, startled. I hurried to the window from which Susie was peering intently into the church parking lot. Sure enough, the wizened little man who had been our neighbor in Thornberry, a four-hour drive away, was climbing out of a taxi, suitcase in hand.

The sight of the taxi itself was so rare in North Doncaster as to seem ominous. It had caught Susie's attention as she glanced out the window on that Saturday morning in late spring. The sight of Alfred added dismay to her surprise.

"What's *he* doing here?" she asked.

"Offhand, I'd say he's planning to visit, though why is beyond me."

"This can't be happening," she muttered to herself. Then, rallying, she added, "You go out and stall him for a few minutes. I'll get the spare room tidied up." She headed off.

As I started out the door, I recalled when, newly ordained and just appointed to the Thornberry Church, I'd first met Alfred Plunket.

Alfred and his wife Dorothy lived across the street from the parsonage, two houses down. In earlier days, the Plunket residence had been a rooming house, used by travelers and seasonal farm laborers. Alfred and Dorothy had made a modest living running the place, Dorothy cooking and cleaning and Alfred handling upkeep and repairs. But the construction of the Interstate highway in the late '50s drew most of the through traffic away from Thornberry, and improvements in harvesting equipment reduced the need for the laborers. The Plunkets were old enough to retire anyway, and they simply closed the business. By the time Susie and I arrived in town, the rooming house had been shut down for nine years, and the couple had the place to themselves.

I'd met Dorothy, a smiling, white-haired woman, at the worship service on my first Sunday. Though a few pounds over her ideal weight and wrinkled with age, she had clearly been a beauty in her younger years. Dorothy had been active in the congregation throughout her lifetime, as was the couple's grown son, who still lived in the community. But although I'd seen Alfred's name on the church's membership role, Dorothy was unaccompanied in church, not only that day, but on each successive Sunday.

Dorothy, I soon discovered, was a woman of sweetness and light, whose Christian virtues shone plainly in her speech, manner, and good works. Each Tuesday morning, Dorothy and a half dozen other older ladies gathered in the fellowship room of the church for quilting. Sitting around the four sides of a large quilting frame, these women industriously stitched their way through three to four quilts every year, quilting them on commission for various customers, and then giving the money to the church's mission fund. The women worked each Tuesday until noon, then ate together from sack lunches they'd brought with them from home.

The quilts they made were beautiful, and I admired them greatly. But as labor-intensive items, they were too expensive for me on a beginning pastor's salary.

Because of the proximity of the Plunket home to ours, I occasionally caught a glimpse of Alfred as he came outside to get into their car. He was shorter than Dorothy, with a bristling shock of dishwater-gray hair, and he walked with a decided limp. But I didn't actually meet Alfred until I made a pastoral visit to their home. Even then, I barely made his acquaintance as he stayed in the living room only long enough to say hello before retreating and leaving Dorothy alone to host me. Dorothy, cheerful and calm, carried on without apology for her husband's brusqueness.

A few weeks later, one of the other quilters filled me in. "Alfred's lived in the township all his life," she said, "but he's always been pretty much a loner. He joined the church back about the time I did, when we were teenagers, but he never attended regularly until he started courting Dorothy. She was a regular attender. Never could understand what she saw in him, though. She was the prettiest girl in our class, and smart and talented too. And you know how nice she is. Alfred was such an odd goat, you know. Never friendly. But once Dorothy made up her mind, she stuck with him."

"He doesn't come to church now, though," I said.

"No, after they'd been married a couple of months, he stopped coming. He's always seemed uncomfortable around people. I figured he forced himself to come while he was pursuing Dorothy, but once he'd married her, he went back to his old ways."

No one else had much to say about Alfred one way or the other. On the other hand, people often mentioned Dorothy, but they spoke about her almost as if she were a widow. Their son, who served on our church board of trustees, was a quiet, steady fellow, but he seldom spoke about Alfred either, though he often referred appreciatively to his mom.

One evening in late fall that first year, I returned from making a hospital visit. Turning into our driveway at dusk, I happened to glance down the street and noticed the Plunket's car parked in front of their house as usual, but its lights were on. It didn't appear that anyone was in it, so I walked the few steps over to it. The engine was not running, but the doors were locked. Assuming Alfred or Dorothy had forgotten to turn off the lights, I stepped onto their porch and knocked on their door. Dorothy answered and I explained.

"Oh, thank you, Reverend Payton," she said. "I went to the store a little while ago. I must have forgotten to turn them off when I got home. I'll take care of it." Because of some vision problems Alfred had developed in his later years, Dorothy now did all the driving.

Later, the phone rang, and when I answered, Dorothy was on the line. "Alfred asked me to call you," she said. "He's sure we'd have had a dead battery in the morning if you hadn't alerted us. He wanted me to thank you again."

"Glad to help," I said, wondering if Alfred was quite as antisocial as I'd thought.

I didn't see Alfred again until midwinter. Actually, I only saw him from behind as he hobbled away from my driveway. In late January, the whole northeastern section of Ohio, including Thornberry, was hit with a blizzard that lasted more than 24 hours. Schools closed and event-cancellations were announced all day long on the radio. When the storm finally ceased, our community was under 17 inches of snow. The township trucks, with snowplows mounted in front, had been working throughout the night, and by morning, when

67

the snow at last stopped falling, the trucks began to make headway, making our streets and roads at least passable.

But my driveway certainly was not. Since first light, I'd been shoveling out, beginning at the garage and working toward the street. The snow was wet and heavy, and the work was exhausting. Still, I gradually cleared a path wide enough for the car to the street. There, I encountered the belt of plowed snow that had been pushed to the side of the street by the township trucks. This massive heap was at least three feet deep, more than four feet wide, and comprised of compressed, hard-packed snow and ice.

Against this massive obstruction my shovel seemed a puny weapon, but I flailed away until some 45 minutes later, I had cleared a passage that I judged to be just wide enough for my car. I had now been at the battle more than three hours. Just as I was beginning to think I could get the car out, a township plow barreled by, widening the traffic lane. In the process, it threw a fresh curl of heavy snow into the end of my driveway. My thoughts at that moment were distinctly unkind.

Though not nearly as wide or deep as the first pile, it took me another 20 minutes of shoveling to undo this latest contribution. Even then, there was still a small hump of tightly packed snow on the ground, but I figured I could get over it with the car if I got a good run from the garage.

At last I was ready to try. I got into the car and began backing out. As I neared the street and prepared to accelerate, I noticed with exasperation that another car was coming slowly down the street. If I gunned the engine now, I'd back right into its path. Reluctantly applying the brakes, I slid to a stop, with the car's rear wheels settling over the icy hump where the driveway met the street.

After the other vehicle passed, I tried to resume backing. The tires spun furiously, but the car had no traction and did not move. I shifted to first gear and attempted to pull back up the drive. Again the tires spun, but the car wouldn't budge. I was stuck.

Retrieving my shovel, I spent the next 30 minutes stabbing at and scraping the resisting mound of snow under the rear tires, but this was the hard-pack, and I made little progress. Every few minutes, I got back in the car and attempted to move it, but to no avail.

Exhausted, with cold feet and an overheated body, I went into the house to recover and get a cup of coffee. Coming back out to try again, I saw Alfred limping back toward his house. His footsteps in the snow led directly to my car, and there, where his tracks turned back, sat an old bucket, filled with sand.

Gratefully, I shoveled generous amounts of the sand under both back tires. This time, when I got in the car and stepped on the accelerator, the tires took hold and my car clawed its way into the street.

I drove to the store and ran a few necessary errands. When I returned, I carried the now empty bucket back to the Plunket's. Dorothy answered my knock, and I expressed my thanks.

She said, "We always kept some sand in case our boarders got their cars stuck, and we still had some." Then, after glancing over her shoulder as if to make sure her husband was out of earshot, she added, "Alfred sat by our window and watched you the whole time you were trying to dig your car out. I think he admires your hard work."

"Uh, thanks," I stammered with surprise.

When warmer weather returned, Susie and I often walked the streets of our neighborhood in the evenings, enjoying the pleasant evening air. But the night I noticed Alfred sitting on his porch, I happened to be walking alone. "Hello," I said.

"Yup," Alfred said, nodding his head. I stopped and made small talk about the weather for a few minutes, and Alfred responded with a few brief comments of his own. "Yup. It is nice."

Susie and I walked by there many evenings after that, but only very occasionally did we encounter Alfred, and then, he was always sitting on his porch. When he was there, we stopped and talked briefly. Alfred never did much with his end of the conversation but I had the feeling that he welcomed our words nonetheless.

Our first child, Tommy, was born a year later, and now when Susie and I walked, we often had Tommy with us, first in stroller and later toddling between us. On the rare occasions when we saw Alfred, he sometimes stuck out his hands to our son. Invariably without hesitation, Tommy went to him. Alfred didn't say much more to Tommy than he did to Susie or me, but clearly the old man enjoyed holding our little boy. That pleased Susie, but she was bothered that Alfred seldom spoke directly to her. She came to think of him as a recluse, and she wondered aloud how Dorothy put up with him.

Following the service on our last Sunday in Thornberry, the congregation held a reception for Susie, Tommy, and me in the church's fellowship hall. Dorothy, although now looking rather frail, was among the women working in the kitchen, laying out the cookies and making the punch. Alfred, of course, was nowhere to be seen.

By August, we were pretty well settled in the North Doncaster parsonage, and I was busy getting to know my new congregation. A phone call from the new seminary graduate who had replaced me in Thornberry brought my attention abruptly back to my former congregation. "Dorothy Plunket died quietly in her sleep last night," he said.

"I'm sorry to hear that," I said. "How's Alfred taking it?"

"That's why I'm calling," he said. "I've never met the man, but their son says his father would like you to perform the funeral. That's okay by me. I'd appreciate it if you would."

So two days later I was back in the Thornberry sanctuary, officiating at the well-attended service for Dorothy. I'd never seen Alfred wearing anything but a flannel shirt and work pants, but today he was clothed in a suit and tie, sitting in the front pew with his son, daughter-in-law, and their family. It occurred to me that this was the first time I'd ever seen him in church. His expression was as somber as I'd ever seen it.

After the funeral and the graveside committal service that followed, Dorothy's family and friends returned to the fellowship hall for a meal served by the women of the church. I too was invited. As we went to the tables, I held back, waiting for the family members to choose their seats. I noticed that while Dorothy's people sat together, Alfred was on the edge of the group. His son sat to Alfred's right, but the seat to his left remained empty. Finally, I took that seat.

"I'm so sorry about Dorothy," I said to Alfred after I was seated.

"Yup," Alfred said. Then, after a pause, he added. "Thanks for doing her funeral. She always liked you."

All of that now swirled in my mind as I walked toward the taxi. "Alfred, this is a surprise." I said. "How are you?"

Alfred gave my extended hand a quick shake, ignoring my question. "I can only stay for three days," he said.

With a guest as untalkative as Alfred, that sounded like an eternity, but I said, "Well, you're welcome."

As he turned to pay the driver, I noted that the cab bore the name Mount Alban, a city some 17 miles away. Alfred pulled out a worn wallet and paid the cabby his stated fee of 35 dollars, and then handed the man an additional 50 cents. The driver looked disgusted, but said nothing. Alfred reached into the cab again and pulled out a second suitcase, this one smaller than the first.

I reached for the larger one, and asked, "How did you get to Mount Alban?"

"I took a bus," Alfred said as the cab drove away.

"Oh. If we'd known you were coming, I could have met you at the station and saved you a cab fare."

"Yup. It cost a lot."

I waited for Alfred to say more, but as usual, he didn't.

"Uh, well ... let's go inside."

As I expected, the next three days were filled with awkward moments as both Susie and I worked hard to maintain a conversation with Alfred. He responded briefly to each of our attempts to begin a dialogue, but soon lapsed back into what seemed to be a contented silence. Tommy was our salvation. Now four years old, he was as talky as Alfred was taciturn, and he kept up a running monologue to which the old man responded with occasional chuckles and expressions like "Yup. Isn't that nice?" and "My, my!" Several times, Tommy climbed into Alfred's lap, yakking away. The first time, Susie, thinking Tommy might be annoying our guest, tried to intervene. But Alfred, in an uncharacteristic spurt of verbosity, said, "No. He's not bothering me. Let him stay. You and I are friends, aren't we, little boy?" Tommy beamed and nodded his head.

That evening, needing to make a trip to the grocery store, I invited Alfred to ride with me. "Okay," he said.

"I bet you miss Dorothy," I said, once we were in the car.

"Yup. She was wonderful."

"I thought so too," I said. Although I waited for Alfred to add more, he remained quiet.

Knowing of Alfred's habitual avoidance of church, I wondered how the next morning, Sunday, would go. "We'll be busy with church tomorrow morning," I said. "We'd love to have you go with us."

"Yup. I'm planning on it."

Sure enough, the next morning Alfred came to breakfast dressed in the same dark gray suit he'd worn to Dorothy's funeral, but said he'd wait until Sunday school was finished before walking over for the worship hour. I wasn't surprised. The adult Sunday school class would no doubt provide more social interaction than a man of Alfred's mindset could tolerate. We left him reading the Sunday paper. As promised, he did appear for worship and sat quietly in the back of the sanctuary.

At dinner, Tommy kept up his chatter at Alfred. We filled the afternoon by driving Alfred to a couple of historic attractions in the area: an old village that had been refurbished by the county historical society and a lock that had been part of the canal system through Ohio in the 19th century. Alfred looked with interest and seemed content. That evening, the old man sat in front of the television, watching it with Tommy in his lap.

As Susie and I lay in bed that night, she said, "You know, I was dreading Alfred being here all weekend, but actually it's been kind of nice. He's really been no trouble at all, and I've enjoyed having him."

We'd arranged that I would drive Alfred to the bus stop the next morning for his trip back to Thornberry. As he prepared to leave the house, he said to Tommy, "Well, goodbye, young man." Tommy solemnly stuck out his hand and Alfred shook it. Alfred then turned to Susie extending his hand, but instead of taking it, she reached out and hugged the old man. He immediately blushed but looked pleased.

He and I said our goodbyes at the bus station. "We're glad you came," I said. "Feel free to come again."

"Yup. Maybe I will. But I'm getting pretty old. You never know." He climbed into the bus.

Later when I got home, Susie met me at the door. "Tom, come with me," she said. "I want to show you something." She led the way to the guestroom where Alfred had slept. There, neatly folded on the bed, lay a beautiful, handmade quilt. A note pinned to it read, "To the Paytons. Dorothy was making this for you."

Three months later, I received a note from the quilter who a few years earlier had told me about Alfred's courtship of Dorothy. Alfred had died peacefully in his sleep, she explained. She added that she hadn't seen the old man since he'd picked up the quilt from them. "Dorothy had started it at home," she wrote. "He brought it to us and paid us to finish it. He never said who it was for, only that it was for some good friends."

14. Jesus Loves Problem Kids

His name was Freddie and he was as cute as little boys come. He was also, according to his Sunday school teacher and the ushers at the North Doncaster church, "a holy terror" who single-handedly disrupted our education and worship times week after week.

Jesus loved him — but after several months of his regular attendance, some of the rest of us weren't so sure that we did.

But still, it was our job to help Freddie know Jesus' love, and, if we were reading the gospel correctly, to be an extension of God's love to him as well.

Although a member of the church, Freddie's single mom hadn't attended in years. Grandma had been bringing Freddie to church with her and had managed some small measure of control over him, but then her health failed, and she could no longer attend. Freddie's mother started dropping him off for the two hours of Sunday school and worship. There, without an adult of his own to supervise him, this little guy ran wild. During class, he monopolized his teacher's attention. During worship, the ushers became his babysitters by default. And more than once, people seated in the sanctuary balcony leapt from their seats to grab Freddie as he careened dangerously near the railing.

We tried all sorts of things. Member families invited him to sit with them, but he'd never stay in their pew for longer than a few minutes. We assigned a teenage helper to his class and during worship gave him several activity sheets and crayons, but none of these efforts was effective for long either.

Finally, we sent a delegation to appeal to his mother to come to church with him, and she did — for one Sunday (during which Freddie behaved angelically). She assumed her single visit had settled the matter and dropped him off on his own again the following Sunday. She ignored our subsequent pleas.

The only suggestion we refused to implement was that we expel Freddie from church. Instead, we struggled along, hoping

Freddie would finally abandon his acting out behavior as he matured. We probably made a lot of mistakes, and child-care experts might have come up with better solutions. But we muddled through.

In his teenage years, Freddie was the livewire of our youth group. He drove more than one adult to distraction with his non-stop clowning and his inevitable testing of the rules. There was nothing mean-spirited in his actions, but it was as if he were driven to act out by some inner hyperactive tormenter. On three occasions I had private talks with Freddie about his disruptive behavior, and each time, he seemed genuinely repentant. But his efforts to reform were always short lived.

Still, we hung in there, and he kept coming to our church events.

By the time Freddie was a young adult, I was no longer at North Doncaster; the bishop had appointed me to another parish. But I'd still hear news from my former church from time to time and eventually word came that Freddie was entering the ministry.

Didn't surprise me one bit.

15. Spring Story

She was dying of pancreatic cancer. "The same kind that got the mayor," she told me in a tone that sounded almost proud. Perhaps she welcomed any measure of identity with somebody prominent, even if only a mutual terminal illness.

"Yep," she said, shifting carefully in her pillow-lined rocking chair, "it hurts me a lot today. And yesterday I couldn't eat. Won't be long 'til I'll be leaving this old place."

Helen Wamsley spoke those words in her usual slip-song rhythm, with no brag at all, and resumed rocking. The gentle spring scent of awakening life blew across her porch where we sat. The breeze should have railed against her matter-of-fact statement that she was soon to die. But curiously, it only whispered acquiescence.

And there was no point in any glib rebuttal from me. Her doctor had predicted fewer than six months remaining, and had signed Helen up for hospice home-care. This county service was available only to the terminally ill, and a hospice nurse came daily to provide routine care.

"I knew 40 years ago cancer would get me some day," Helen said, still rocking slowly. "That's what my Annie died of, don't you know." This last she pronounced as *duntchano*. I'd gotten used to her habit of tacking this litany onto statements of fact — or those Helen believed were factual — so I knew she was not expecting a response. Annie, I'd learned during my first visit, was Helen's daughter, the sweet-faced 9-year-old who lived now only in the faded black-and-white photo on the mantle in Helen's living room, and in Helen's memory.

Helen had already passed her thirty-sixth birthday when Annie was born. "For a time, Everett and me thought the good Lord wasn't going to let us have any young ones," Helen had said, "but then Annie came." Everett had been killed a few years later in a railroad accident. Until the child's death, Helen supported the two of them by working as a school cook. Afterward, she worked another eight years on that job until a school consolidation eliminated the position. She spent the balance of her working career as a grade-school

77

crossing guard, continuing until school rules forced her to retire at age 80.

"I still miss Annie someti—." A freight train rumbled slowly by on the tracks barely 100 yards from Helen's door. Acting on the habit instilled by long residency beside this source of racket, Helen automatically paused in mid-speech until the train passed, and by then, her thoughts seemed to have turned another direction.

She pointed to an old maple tree near the corner of her lot. "Funny about that tree. Only one around here that loses its leaves in the spring 'stead of the fall, don't you know."

I glanced where she'd pointed. The thick buds on the tree looked ready to open any day, but a number of dead leaves lay on the ground beneath it, and looked recently fallen. "Surely they don't stay green all winter," I said.

"Course not. They dry up and turn brown in autumn like all the other leaves. They just don't fall, not even when the winter winds blow, not even under the weight of snow, don't you know. Nope, they hang on all winter until the growing edge of the new buds knocks them loose in the spring. I figure the old leaves are protecting the buds underneath."

"It's kind of sad to see dead leaves in springtime," I said.

"No, it's not. They've finished their job. It's all right." Abruptly she returned to her previous subject. "Let me tell you how dangerous that radiation stuff is. Just being near somebody being treated with it can kill a person, don't you know."

"Well, if used improperly —"

"Don't make much difference either way. It didn't save Annie, and it got me instead."

"But you haven't been exposed to radiation, Helen." She'd already told me that radiation therapy hadn't been an option in her case; the cancer had been too far advanced before diagnosis. Her doctor hadn't even suggested radiation therapy, but Helen had made it clear she'd have nothing to do with it anyway.

"Yes, I *was* exposed," Helen said firmly. "Radiation got me while Annie was treated, and it's been sneaking up on me ever since."

My curiosity was piqued. Annie had died before my time, when radiation therapy was in a primitive stage. Still, as far as I knew, shielded rooms were in use by then, with everybody but the patient excluded. "How were you exposed, Helen?"

" 'Cause I sat in the room with Annie." A defiant note crept into Helen's voice. "They made me wait outside the first time, but Annie was scared. She kept crying for me. It like to broke my heart. I told them that if they didn't let me stay in with her, they wasn't treating her no more. So they gave in."

"Did they warn you of the risk?"

"Sure they did. But it didn't matter. I was going to be with Annie. She needed me." Helen sat up very tall, but then sagged, wincing with pain. Something in her spirit suddenly sagged too, as she quietly added, "Course, it was all for nothing. Annie died anyway." I waited for the "don't you know," but for once, Helen left that appendage off. Appropriately so, I decided: No one could know exactly what painful emotions she was now reliving.

Allowing Helen to remain in the room during Annie's therapy had been a serious breach of safety rules. Although the beam would have been aimed at the daughter, the mother probably received secondary radiation. I'd read somewhere about the danger. As rays enter the patient's body, some diverge because of collision with the body tissues. They fly off in all directions. Helen could be right about the cause of her cancer, for radiation's effects are cumulative. Exposure can cause irreversible damage, though it may take years to show.

But I saw suddenly that it didn't matter whether she was accurate or not; Helen's reality was what she believed. She had believed she was risking her life to sit with Annie, and had done it willingly.

"You must have loved her very much," I said.

"Yes," she said quietly.

"You look tired, Helen. Would you like to go inside and lie down for a while?"

"I would."

I helped the old woman slowly to her feet, trying to avoid causing her additional pain. Holding my arm, she took three small steps toward the door, and then turned and looked for a few seconds at the landscape, drinking in the spring scene. Her eyes lingered briefly on the corner of her yard.

"Funny about that tree," she said.

16. The Other Roads

In the course of my ministry I occasionally came upon people who had gone rather suddenly from being enthusiastic believers to functional nonbelievers. But for as often as I encountered such disheartened souls, only once was I actually an eyewitness to the fall.

Harold, in his mid-fifties, stood tall in our congregation, both physically and spiritually. Well over six feet tall, with a full head of dark wavy hair going silver at the temples, he was striking to look at. But his faith was also handsome to behold. With his buoyant personality and upbeat outlook on life, Harold was a strong leader in our congregation, a man I thought of as an "encourager." He talked openly about his faith, without being obnoxious or pushy, and cheered others on in theirs.

He owned an insurance office, a one-man agency, but one that did a strong business, thanks in no small part to Harold's winsome personality. His unsinkable outlook also made him a good teacher, and he taught our young-adult Sunday school class. More than one of the class members sought him out for advice about their lives, and none were disappointed in the help they received from him.

Part of what made Harold a strong model of a believer was how he had handled the sudden death of his wife, Margie. During my second year at North Doncaster, Margie, driving home one evening from the grocery store, was hit head-on by a drunk driver and killed instantly. Harold was devastated, but remained an anchor of courage for his family and the couple's friends. The congregation closed in around Harold, like the sheltering wing of a mother hen, providing strong support. When Harold emerged from the tragedy, he was a sadder man, but his faith was intact.

Harold and Margie had had two children: a daughter, Nancy, and a son, Doug. They'd provided a Christian atmosphere in their home, and I'd been told that they'd brought both kids with them to church from the time they were born. In his late teen years, however, Doug had dropped out. There's an irony that's fairly common in families with strong church backgrounds — offspring who don't include the church in their adult lives. Nancy, two years older than

Doug, had married within the community and remained an active member of the congregation. Doug, however, had gone his own way. He'd lurched through what Harold called a "wild period" in his late teens and early adulthood — fast cars, motorcycles, alcohol, some minor scrapes with the law — but eventually he'd matured out of that. Doug never took his father up on the offer to pay for college, but settled into a factory job, living and working in a community some 25 miles from North Doncaster. In time, he married Hannah, and the pair had two little girls, whom Harold bragged about regularly.

Doug's new problem began mildly enough — a few seemly stupid mistakes at work, occasional headaches, some almost comical forgetfulness. But eventually these things were understood as symptoms, and the verdict was a brain tumor.

All of which led us — Harold, Nancy, Hannah, and I — to be in the hospital waiting room, anticipating the surgeon's report. The X-rays and other tests beforehand, while verifying the presence of the tumor, hadn't given a definitive answer. We wouldn't know the full extent of the tumor's reach, nor the prognosis for Doug, until the surgeon actually opened Doug's skull. We clung together in hope.

When the surgeon came in, we all stood, anxious to hear the news.

It was about as bad as it could be. Doug had survived the surgery, and some cancerous material had been removed, but what remained was interlaced into Doug's brain. He might live a few months, the surgeon said, a couple of them with relative normalcy, thanks to what had been removed, but that was the best that could be hoped for.

That was the moment, I believe, when something caved in inside Harold. He seemed dazed. I gripped his arm while Hannah and Nancy embraced him, and they all wept.

After the doctor left the room, we sank down to our chairs. I was directly across from Harold, watching him intently, worrying about him. I saw his shoulders sag as the weight of the news crashed in on him.

And that's when the chair collapsed beneath him. All at once, it simply fell apart, and Harold, still on the seat cushion, dropped to the floor. Startling though this was, he seemed not to notice. His world had fallen apart. That the same thing should happen to his chair was not worth registering.

We all rushed to his assistance. Seeing that he was unhurt, we helped him to his feet and lowered him into another chair.

Later, as I was leaving the hospital, I saw a hospital maintenance man and mentioned the chair to him. "Hmm," he murmured, "never had that happen before."

The possible two months of normalcy never happened. Doug regained consciousness after a few hours and we all talked to him briefly. Two days later, he went into a crisis and died. Harold had remained at the hospital with his son since the surgery and was at Doug's bedside through it all. He was holding Doug's hand as the young man breathed his last.

I conducted Doug's funeral on Thursday, and Harold moved through the day responding to friends and fellow mourners naturally and with grace, but the spark was gone from him. On Sunday, nobody expected Harold to come and teach his class, and without asking him, we arranged for a substitute teacher. Harold did not come for worship either. On Monday, though, I heard he had re-opened his insurance office, and I stopped in to see him. Harold, looking somehow shrunken, greeted me in a friendly manner, but I could tell he did not want to talk about his grief.

He was not present for any of the next three Sundays at church, but on the fourth one, he came for worship, though not to teach his class. He went through the motions of the service, standing when we stood, bowing his head during prayer, dropping a check in the offering. But during the singing of the hymns, he stood mutely, looking lost in thought, or maybe just lost. Two days later, I got a note from Harold asking to be permanently relieved of his teaching responsibility.

Over the next few months, Harold came to church only very occasionally. I visited him a few times. He was unfailingly polite, but I sensed that he was locked behind a wall of grief. Nancy, handling her own grief, told me that her father was more remote than she'd ever seen him, and she worried about him constantly.

But though Harold walked in the valley of the shadow, life around him went on. Doug's little girls had birthdays, and Harold went to their house to help them celebrate. As an insurance agent, Harold had made sure Doug and Hannah had good coverage, so Hannah was able to retain their house, but she still struggled financially without Doug's income. Harold was there often to help with household repairs, and several times he quietly handed Hannah a check to help with expenses. And then, four month's after Doug's death, Nancy, who had been childless throughout her 12 years of marriage, discovered she was pregnant. It was Harold who told me that news, though he delivered it in a flat, matter-of-fact tone. I feared for his well-being.

That was the same conversation during which Harold confessed he could not pray any more. "My prayers don't go anywhere," he said. "Maybe they never did."

"What's the alternative?" I asked.

"I don't know," Harold said, shaking his head.

It's a truism that time heals, but it's also a graciousness of life, and slowly, with the support of his family and friends, Harold began to claw his way out of deepest troughs of despair. What brought him back to church were his granddaughters. Hannah had begun to talk about her girls needing some religious education. She worked most Sundays, so Harold volunteered to bring them to Sunday school. Each Sunday, he picked them up and delivered them to our church building. After making sure they got to their classrooms, he drove to a nearby café, where he drank coffee and read the paper. He returned in time for the worship service, and sat through it with the girls.

We had recruited a permanent replacement to teach the young-adult class. One Sunday, a full 16 months after Doug's funeral, that teacher had another obligation, but was unable to find a substitute. Finally, she asked Harold, and after some hesitation, he accepted.

As it happened, I was present in the class that morning. Although I usually attended another adult class, I occasionally visited other classes. And this morning, quite unaware that Harold was subbing, I dropped in on the young adults.

I was surprised and pleased to see him there, and glad for how warmly the class members welcomed him back.

Harold began tentatively, but soon moved smoothly into the lesson, a study on one of the Old Testament prophets. He concluded it with about five minutes to spare. Putting the lesson book aside, he said, "I'd like to tell you something I've learned these last months. All of you know the things that have happened in my family. After Doug died, so soon after I lost Margie, I fell into a black hole. I've never known such pain. I couldn't pray, I couldn't find any comfort ... For the first time in my life, I wondered if there really was a God, or if there was, that perhaps he was unfair or cruel, not to be trusted. A customer of mine asked me why I didn't just chuck this whole faith business and turn to something else."

His words gripped the attention of the class members. No one stirred as they waited for him to continue.

"But turn to what? Our pastor here," he said, nodding in my direction, "asked me the same thing in another way. He asked me what was the alternative, and that question has haunted me these last months. I don't begin to understand this life as I once thought I did. I know that in the past some of you have asked me for advice, and I may have too easily suggested that there were answers in our faith. I think I see now that faith isn't about answers. All I can tell you now is that for me at least, there is no alternative. The other roads go nowhere."

No one spoke. After a moment, a young woman rose from her seat and walked toward Harold. Leaning over, she embraced him. Other class members joined her, and soon Harold was surrounded by the students.

From that time on, Harold remained with the congregation, attending worship most Sundays, usually with his granddaughters in tow. Now, instead of dropping them off and heading for the café, he began attending the Sunday school class for his age group. And when needed, he'd substitute for the young-adult class. He was a quieter man now, one tested in the fire. He'd been an encourager. Now he was something more: a man by whom many measured their lives — and their faith.

17. Strangers

When Betty appeared at my door she looked positively ill. It was 6:30 on a Friday evening and the rehearsal for her daughter's wedding was to begin in a half hour. "The wedding's off!" she blurted when I opened the door.

I was surprised, but I instantly recognized that for Betty this was a catastrophe. In most weddings, the mother of the bride invests herself emotionally, but in this case, it had gone way beyond that.

I invited her in and asked what happened.

Betty sighed wearily. "Liz has changed her mind," she said, shaking her head. "She got home from Europe two days ago, and Tony came in last night. They've been apart for nearly three months, and now she says they feel like strangers."

"I can see how that could happen."

"Yes, but what a mess! Bill and I have just been on the phone for hours — we had people flying in from all over the country. We tried to catch them in time to cancel their flights. We got some, but others are already in the air. And we canceled the cake, the flowers, the musicians, the reception hall ... everything. It's a disaster! And we're still going to have to pay for a lot of it anyway — though that's the least of it." Betty looked as if she would cry.

Liz and Tony had met in college and dated since their freshman year. They'd become engaged a year ago. In their senior year, Liz had had an opportunity to study for a semester in France. Tony had stayed on campus to finish his degree, but they'd planned to marry upon Liz's return — a full church wedding, complete with lots of bridesmaids, ushers, a bevy of relatives from both families, and loads of friends. Since Liz would not be home to make the arrangements, Betty had agreed to handle them, and had done a magnificent job at it. She'd been a very busy lady for the last three months.

And now, everything was falling apart.

"So I'm here to cancel the rehearsal and the wedding itself," Betty said to me. "I'm terribly sorry."

"There's nothing to be sorry for. This is no trouble for me. I feel badly for you and Bill, though. I know you've worked hard on this. How does Tony feel?"

"He's stunned. But the three month's apart ... We were all proud of Liz getting the scholarship ... but now I'm not so sure it was a good thing." Betty placed her hand on her chest as if stilling her heart. "I can't believe this is happening!"

We talked for a couple of minutes more. Then Betty headed for home to make some final phone calls. I walked into the living room to tell Susie what had happened.

The time of the rehearsal came and went. Susie and I went for an evening walk, and then returned home. At about 10:15, Betty appeared at my door again. She'd looked sick before; she now appeared to be frantic as well.

"Liz has changed her mind again! They want to go ahead with the wedding! Is it too late?"

"Not as far as I'm concerned. The church is still available. What happened?"

"Liz and Tony had a long talk, and she seems okay now. It was just the separation. Liz panicked, I think," Betty said.

"It happens. But I bet they'll be okay. Back when I met with them before Liz went to France, I was impressed by how mature they both seemed."

"I wish they'd gotten back together sooner. I don't know how much of this I can take. We've all been on the phones again. It's too late for the cake and the caterer, and the original flowers were sold to someone else. I had to get the florist at home. They're trying to scrounge something up. Fortunately the hall was still available."

"What about the relatives?"

"That's the worst part. A lot of them had already canceled flights and don't have time to get here now. Not even all the wedding party can make it. But I guess we'll go with who we've got, if it's all right with you."

"Fine with me."

And so it was that at 11:30 that night, we had the rehearsal at the church. Three of the five bridesmaids were there, and two of the ushers. The maid of honor would arrive in time for the wedding itself, so we practiced around her vacant spot. The best man hadn't been able to get another flight, so one of the ushers was pressed into service.

Tony looked rattled, but Liz, carrying herself erect, appeared radiant. She had taken a moment when she first got to the church to apologize to me for the off-again, on-again start, and I'd gathered that she'd also apologized to the wedding party members. "But I couldn't go ahead with all those doubts," she'd said to me. "I'm sorry for the big mess, and for what I put Mom and Dad through. But I feel better about getting married now."

The next day, the wedding itself went smoothly, though only about half of the originally invited guests were present. With the caterer canceled, the women of the church rushed to Betty's rescue, preparing food for the reception and helping to serve it, so that part too worked out.

Tony had landed a job in another state, and after the honeymoon, the couple moved there. I only saw them occasionally when they came back to North Doncaster to visit Betty and Bill.

The last time Liz and Tony were home, they and their six children appeared to be very happy.

18. Generations

The ringing phone woke us out of a deep sleep. I scrabbled for the receiver. "Hello?" I mumbled.

"Reverend Payton? It's Tiffany. I'm sorry to call so late." The young woman sounded weepy.

"That's all right. What's wrong?"

"Justin's left me. He just walked out."

"I'm sorry to hear that." I was becoming fully awake.

"I don't know what to do."

Realizing this wasn't going to be a quick call, I told Tiffany I needed to switch phones. Susie was eight months pregnant with our second child, and I didn't want to keep her awake unnecessarily. Tommy was almost 7, and we'd begun to think Susie would not conceive again. Then she discovered herself with child, and we both rejoiced. I handed her the receiver and asked her to hang it up once I'd picked up downstairs.

Pulling on my bathrobe, I staggered down the stairs, thinking about the couple. Justin and Tiffany, both in their late twenties, were members of my church, as were Tiffany's parents and grandparents. Justin hadn't grown up in the church, but had joined shortly after he and Tiffany married. And he'd become a hard-working member, eventually serving on the Board of Trustees and performing usher duties during Sunday services.

But for reasons that I could never figure out, Tiffany's mother, Margaret, didn't like the young man. She'd been against the marriage from the start, although once Tiffany made it clear she was going through with it, her mother threw herself into the wedding preparations.

Nonetheless, Margaret continued to find fault with Justin, and Tiffany, who was close to her mother, often felt caught in the middle.

Once on the other line, I asked Tiffany what had happened.

"Another fight," she said, her voice breaking. "But a really big one this time. Mom got Grandpa to offer Justin a job. It would have been a better salary, but Justin didn't want it. I guess I kind of pressured him to take it. But he wouldn't. He got really mad at me."

From past experience with the couple, I could envision what Tiffany meant by "pressured." She wasn't a nagger, but if the argument followed a course similar to previous ones I'd helped them untangle, she had tried to "reason" with Justin, doggedly laying down statement after statement about why Justin should accept the offer. And at least some of those statements would have started with, "Mom thinks ..." And they'd have rolled roughshod over Justin's protestations that he already had a job, one in the career path he wanted to pursue.

Like many young couples, Justin and Tiffany had financial problems. A better salary would have been welcome, but I knew money wasn't really the primary cause of the current disagreement. It wasn't even Margaret's interference, but Tiffany's unwillingness to establish enough independence from her.

I could also guess that Tiffany's marshaled arguments included the statement that her grandfather had been generous in proffering the job, and that she didn't want to offend him by Justin's refusal of the offer. I'd refereed disputes between the couple involving similar scenarios before and had helped them look at the roots of their problems. But of course, looking at them and modifying deeply ingrained behavior were two different things.

Justin, despite his basic decency, wasn't the sort to ease tension. Quick to anger and sharply critical of his wife, he'd have quickly flamed up as Tiffany battered him with reason after reason why he should acquiesce. He'd stormed out of the house before, but Tiffany's statement this time that "Justin's left me," was a first, and suggested that matters had reached a new low.

Listening to Tiffany now on the phone, I heard a child's cry in the background. "Are the boys up?" I asked.

"Yes, the argument woke up Kyle, and he woke up Jess."

"Well, you need to get them settled again. There's not much we can do tonight. Why don't you come in to the church tomorrow, and we can talk further then? I could see you around 10:00. Will that work?"

Tiffany said it would, but launched into a retelling of the argument. I let her go for a couple of minutes, but eventually insisted she get her boys back to sleep. That seemed to finally get through to her.

Once back in bed, my mind wouldn't shut off. "Grandpa" was Margaret's father, Owen. He owned a successful lumber business and, along with his wife, Maribeth, had been "pillar" members of the congregation for years. The whole family was highly respected in the community and the church.

It was not a misplaced respect either, for they were good people, but through my involvement with Justin and Tiffany, I had a view of a family dynamic most outsiders didn't see.

Initially, when Tiffany and Justin had first come to me to help them through a marital rough spot, I'd tried to help them examine how they communicated, both verbally and in the more subtle ways warring couples jab each other. I thought they'd made some progress. But when their relationship hit more trouble, the understanding they'd gained didn't seem to serve them very well.

As Margaret's complicity in their problems became clear, I began to think of their difficulties as involving two generations. I'd talked at length with both Tiffany and Justin about what they needed to do to maintain a healthy separation between Margaret's expectations and their own goals. But while Tiffany supposedly understood and agreed, she was unable to put her understanding into action for very long. When Margaret spoke up, Tiffany, even while arguing with her mother, was also getting "hooked" again by the power of Margaret's personality.

The longer I worked with the couple, the more I understood that their problems played out on a larger arena, involving not two but three generations. From everything I knew, neither Owen nor Maribeth was ever directly involved in any of Justin and Tiffany's spats. If anything, they steered clear of the conflict and tried to maintain a friendly relationship with both their granddaughter and her husband. Their complicity — especially Owen's — in the couple's deepening woes was behind the scenes. Owen, who apparently liked Justin, still thought him not motivated enough to seize opportunity and shared his opinion with Margaret. Owen himself, when Justin's age, had arrived in the community nearly penniless, and within a few short years had founded his business and built it to financial success.

As near as I could tell, Margaret's relationship with her father was based on genuine admiration for him. Clearly, he had been actively involved in his daughter's life while she was growing up, and, based on how often Margaret quoted Owen's self-confident advice, she still considered him a strong figure in her life. Too strong perhaps. Whenever I'd heard Margaret refer to her dad, her tone became almost submissive — very different from the forceful manner she adopted with Tiffany.

Margaret's relationship with her husband, Ted, revealed yet another view of her personality. It was obvious to me that while Owen and Ted respected each other, Ted had early on established boundaries around his own household, which Owen accepted. Ted and Margaret's relationship, it seemed to me, was that of equals.

In Owen's view, Margaret had married well, and if Ted was an independent thinker who insisted Owen stay out of his marriage, that was fine. Ted, so I'd heard Owen say, had life "well in hand."

Ted viewed Tiffany's and Justin's problems as "just between them," and though he knew of his wife's involvement in their arguments, he saw his role as one of peacemaker, trying to smooth things over between his wife and daughter. Unfortunately, his efforts were like trying to stop a hemorrhage with a Band-Aid.

When Tiffany arrived at the church in the morning, she told me she had called Justin's workplace and found him there. He'd reported for work as usual. On the phone, she asked him to come home after work, but Justin said he didn't think he would. "We have no future," he'd said plainly.

Tiffany had left the boys with her mother so she could come to talk with me, and while dropping them off, she had filled her mother in on the battle the night before. Tiffany told me that Margaret's response had been, "If Justin doesn't come back, it might be for the best."

We talked for a while. Tiffany started describing the argument in detail. When I pushed her to look beyond the "he-said-I-said" account at the larger issues, she tried, but I could sense a weariness in her that seemed to block comprehension.

And then we were interrupted by my secretary knocking on the door, an unusual occurrence during counseling. "I'm sorry to

94

cut in," she said, "but Susie called. She's in labor and says you should come home right away."

I told Tiffany we'd have to continue our discussion later, and she agreed I should hurry home.

Our daughter Jenny was born nine hours later, a little premature, but with other problems as well. She was a beautiful girl, but we never got to bring her home from the hospital. Susie and I spent days and days with her there, but after eight weeks little Jenny died.

We were heartbroken, and though I tried to be strong for Susie, I hurt deeply. The congregation was supportive, helping out with Tommy, sending in meals, praying for us, and insisting that I take some time off from parish duties. Owen stopped by to offer his condolences and told me of a child he and Maribeth had lost in the early years of their marriage. "I thought for a while I wouldn't get through it," he said, "but I had to. Maribeth needed me and so did Margaret." Somehow I found the old man's visit especially comforting.

During that time, Justin sued for divorce, which Tiffany did not contest. They shared custody of their boys, but Kyle and Jess spent most of their time with Tiffany, and thus with Margaret and Ted, and with Owen and Maribeth. When the boys were teens, they both worked after school in Owen's lumberyard. Kyle loved it, and Owen, who was already in his seventies, began grooming Kyle to take over the business. Jess, however, had a different temperament, and pursued other interests. His inattentiveness at the yard made him the object of Owen's disapproval time and again, and during one scolding, Owen said, "You're just like your father. It's too bad." Or at least that's what Jess heard.

Who can say if Owen's attitude toward those who didn't match his idea of hard work had anything to do with trouble Jess got into later? After a spree involving drugs and car theft, Jess spent six months in county jail. Jess never blamed anyone but himself, but he once told me, "I could never please my great-grandfather."

In more than one place in the Old Testament, there is a reference to God "visiting" the sin of parents upon their children and their children's children, even as far as the fourth generation. I had always found them difficult words to understand, but gradually, as I worked with multigenerational families, I began to get a glimmer of what that meant. In the Old Testament era, families lived together in clans, with the eldest male in absolute charge. Given normal lifespans, four generations is about all that would be alive and dwelling together at any one time, and thus all that would be affected by actions, be they good or bad, of the patriarch. But such was the power of the male elder that his decisions sat heavily on all four generations in his camp.

But who can trace with absolute certainty cause and effect through a chain of human relationships? All I know is that when people ask me to counsel them, I am never sure how many generations enter my study when the counselee walks in.

19. Still Standing

"What I need," said the man who'd come to my door, "is for a pastor to offer a prayer and then do nothing more. Do you understand?"

I didn't care much for his instruct-the-help tone, but I invited him in. "Why do you want me at all, then?" I asked.

The well-dressed man had come requesting my participation at a funeral. He'd introduced himself as Robert Drake. The deceased, a retired veterinarian whom I'd never met, was to be memorialized and buried two days hence, and according to Mr. Drake, a minister was required for a prayer. Any eulogizing would be taken care of by his friends.

"If it were up to me," he said bluntly, "you wouldn't be there. But don't worry, you'll be well paid even though your participation will be minimal."

"I wasn't worried. If I agree, it won't have anything to do with money. I'm willing to offer a prayer for any man's life, but I'd like to understand what's going on here."

Drake looked annoyed. "John had no use for religion, and I'd just as soon send him off without any holy mumbo-jumbo." Clearly he wasn't concerned about sparing my sensibilities. "But it's not entirely up to me. I was John's friend and now I'm his executor. I'm making the funeral arrangements ... but I do have to contend with a few of our mutual friends who think it's not a funeral without some preacher praying."

"So I'm the compromise?"

"That's about the size of it. So you'll do it?"

When I didn't respond immediately, his look of annoyance shifted to what seemed to be distress. "Look," he said, "you're the third minister I've asked. I haven't got time to go running all over looking for somebody to pray. Isn't this part of your job, praying for the dead?"

"At the moment, I'm more interested in the living. I'm not surprised that my colleagues have turned you down. Why are you so angry about religion?"

"That's none of your business. I can see I'll have to go elsewhere." He started to rise.

"I'll come and pray, Mr. Drake, but on one condition."

Drake stiffened. "What condition?"

"That you tell me about John. Tell me what was important to him, what he valued ... why you and he were friends."

I could see Drake weighing his options. He probably didn't have time to run all over. Besides, there were only three ministers in our small town, including me.

"You're not leaving me much choice," Drake said. He glanced at his watch. "I guess I can spare a few minutes. But why do you care about John? He hasn't lived around here since he was a kid."

I thought of the many times I'd conducted funerals for total strangers. Usually those requests came from funeral directors trying to accommodate families left to make the "arrangements" for someone who'd died without a church connection. Funerals for members of my church, while sometimes difficult emotionally, were not hard to prepare, for I could speak from personal acquaintance about them, talking about their faith, commitment, love of their family, service in the church, and so forth. Sometimes I knew of touching or even humorous incidents from a person's life. But services for people unknown to me were more difficult. There was no point of connection, and I was forced to speak in generalities about the biblical perspective on life and death.

But none of that was why I'd asked Drake to discuss his friend. "It's useful to hear you talk about him," I said.

Drake began, "Well, as I said, he was my friend ... my best friend, actually. We met in college." He went on to describe a friendship based in part on common interests and mutual respect, but more on the fact that John, although only a year older than Drake, had been a mentor of sorts to him. Regarding religion, Drake said, his friend had been "a freethinker" with little use for what couldn't be empirically demonstrated.

John had cared about animals, not just professionally through his career, but on a personal level as well. He'd been active in an animal-rights group, and in fact, had requested that donations be made to that organization in lieu of flowers at his funeral.

98

Drake had begun talking tentatively, and I had to ask prompting questions a couple of times to keep him moving. But now he was warming up to talking about this man he obviously respected. "I guess the best way to describe him was as a caring man — animals, people ... me. He cared about us all."

"Can you recall an example of when you felt really cared for by John?" I asked.

"Of course, lots of them. Look, is this really necessary?"

"If you would, please."

"Well, I guess the time that sticks in my mind most was while my wife was dying. Cancer. In just seven months, Jane went from being a healthy woman in the prime of life to a shadow of herself. John was there for me all the time."

"That's the mark of a good friend."

"Which is more than I can say for your God!" These words erupted suddenly from Drake's lips. "Where was he when I needed him? I prayed every day for Jane, but it did no good."

I waited in silence for his emotion to subside a bit. Then I said, "Perhaps you need to forgive God."

He looked surprised, and then stood up abruptly. "I've done as you've asked. You'll come and do the prayer, as you agreed?"

I told him I would.

He told me the time and place, and then quickly made his exit.

The day of John's funeral came, and I listened intently as three of his friends spoke, one after the other, of John's good works and excellent friendship. Afterward, I offered the prayer, thanking God for the man and the compassionate life he had led. We then drove in procession to the cemetery.

Following the graveside committal, Drake approached me. Holding out an envelope, he spoke formally. "Thank you for coming and praying. Several of our friends mentioned that they appreciated what you said." He thrust the envelope forward.

"You're welcome." Glancing at the envelope, I added. "Please give whatever's in there to the animal-rights group John supported."

Drake looked surprised, but finally said, "All right."

I shook his hand and turned to walk toward my car.

"Uh ... Just a minute, Reverend."

I turned around. "Yes?"

"What you said — about my forgiving God — that didn't make sense. I thought your religion says *we* need *God's* forgiveness?"

"We do. But sometimes we need the healing that comes from forgiving him."

"I don't understand."

Feeling suddenly weary, I exhaled deeply. "I'm not sure I can explain it any better than that. A lot of us would like to know why loved ones suffer as they do — and there are Christians who say that someday, from the perspective of eternity, it will make some kind of sense. I don't know if that's so or just wishful thinking. But either way, that doesn't help us here when we are in pain."

"So what good does faith do then?"

I noticed a bird hopping on the top of a nearby tombstone, and cast my eyes in its direction. "I can only tell you that faith ... sometimes ... well, sometimes it gives us something we need to go on without ... without being poisoned by what has happened." I glanced toward Drake. "And our refusal to forgive God interferes with that."

"So you're saying I need to forgive God for taking Jane from me?"

"It's a place to start," I said, continuing to watch the bird.

Drake didn't say anything to that, but stood there eyeing me intently for a moment. Finally he said, "You've had to do that too, haven't you? You've had to forgive God."

I looked back at Drake. "Yes," I said quietly. "We lost a daughter."

Drake and I stood there silently together for a long minute, both watching the bird as it hopped on the granite marker to some unmetered rhythm only it could hear.

Finally, Drake reached over and gripped my shoulder.

I nodded.

Then he turned around and walked back to rejoin his friends still standing around the open grave.

20. Resurrection

Up until this incident, Lucille Brennan would have said that the day she was approved to be a foster parent was the happiest one of her life. For there, at last, at age 57, she'd finally been declared fit to mother little children, and she even had an official letter from the county Department of Children's Services to prove it.

It's not that she'd never been a mother before, but that she'd never been a very good one. As a young woman, she'd given birth to a boy she named Joe, but the circumstances hadn't been advantageous.

Already by then, Lucille had led a life she didn't feel good about. There was no husband on the scene, and she wasn't absolutely sure who Joe's father was. She loved her little boy, but, trying to make it on her own was hard. She often let little Joe fend for himself while she worked to earn a few dollars as a barmaid. Sometimes she earned a little more from the men who frequented the bar, but of course she couldn't have Joe around while she entertained them. Joe ended up spending way too much time by himself.

Then, too, Lucille drank too much in those days. By the time Joe was 6, he'd gotten used to finding his mother passed out on the sofa.

Remarkably, he turned out to be one of those kids who, despite a lousy background, manage to stay out of trouble. He had enough gumption to pay attention in school and learn his lessons. But at 16, he moved in with a friend. Asked if he'd miss his mother, he said, "Nah. She's never had time for me anyway. She'll hardly know I'm gone."

In some ways that was almost true, but of course, Lucille did miss Joe, and when she was honest with herself, she was ashamed of how poor a mother she had been to him. At first, she tried to see Joe once in a while, but he made it clear that he wanted no further contact. So she'd finally let the relationship go.

Things had gone on like that for several years. By the time Lucille, at age 54, found Jesus, she hadn't seen Joe for more than a dozen years. In fact, he hadn't stayed in touch and she now had no idea where he was.

Lucille had let Christ into her life as a result of the efforts of one of her few friends, a woman named Eileen, a member of our church. Several times Eileen had invited Lucille to come to church with her, and finally, one Sunday when Lucille couldn't think of any reason not to go, she came. To her surprise, she was touched by the service that morning, and she began to attend regularly. In time, through the constant acceptance and friendship she found in our church, Lucille gave her heart to Jesus and really began to change her life.

I guess I'm responsible for planting the idea that Lucille become a foster mother. After services one Sunday, she lingered to talk with me about the guilt she still felt because of how she'd wasted her life and how she'd been such a poor mother to her son. She was looking for a way to make up for that. I assured her that God had forgiven her past and that she wasn't required to make up for it. But when she persisted, I suggested that she check out the foster-parent program. "They're always looking for people to house kids from problem homes," I said.

"Do you think they'd let me, I mean, with my background?"

"I don't know. But you're a new person now, and I'll be glad to vouch for you."

That's how it came about that Lucille, after being thoroughly checked out by the Department of Children's Services, had arrived at her happy day when she'd been okayed for duty as a foster parent.

And that's also why members of our congregation started speaking about "Lucille's brood." For now, every Sunday when she arrived at church, two or three and occasionally even four little children trooped along behind her. Sometimes she even had a baby in her arms. Clearly, Lucille was in her glory.

Foster parenting being what it is, some children were only with her a few weeks while their home situations were being resolved or while adoptions were worked out. Others stayed several months, and one little girl had been with her from the beginning of her foster parenting. I knew the director of the Department of Children's Services, and she told me that they considered Lucille one of their better foster parents.

So I wasn't surprised when the department asked Lucille to take one of their sadder cases. The baby, the worker explained to Lucille, was a boy, 5 months old, named Jimmy. He'd been born to a teenage mother and her live-in boyfriend. The boyfriend, intolerant of the baby's crying and fussing, had beaten the child unmercifully several times, until finally, the mother had reported him and he'd been arrested. By then, Jimmy had been emotionally damaged as well. "He doesn't cry anymore," the worker said. "He just lays there in his crib, silently."

"Bring him," Lucille said.

When Jimmy arrived, it was just as the worker had said. Jimmy, a beautiful little boy, though frighteningly thin and pale, did not cry when he was hungry, or wet, or cold, or in any sort of discomfort. Lucille noticed that he occasionally whimpered quietly, but that was all.

At this time, Lucille already had two other children in her home, a toddler and a 5-year-old. They required attention too, but it seemed important to Lucille that Jimmy be held, and held a lot. And so for weeks, whatever Lucille was doing, she did one-handed. Her other arm was busy cradling Jimmy, who remained as silent as ever. When she needed two hands, she fashioned a large towel into a sling, and carried Jimmy in it, across her stomach.

Jimmy wouldn't cry to tell her when he was hungry, so Lucille made it a point to feed him on a regular schedule, to make sure he was not undernourished. Gradually color began to return to the child's cheeks and he gained a little weight ... but he did not cry.

Of course, when Sunday came, Jimmy went to church with Lucille and the other two children. Our entire congregation soon heard the story of this latest addition to Lucille's brood. Eileen had already put Jimmy on the church's prayer chain.

As often as she could, Lucille sat with Jimmy in her arms and rocked him, singing lullabies to him in quiet tones.

And so it went. Lucille would get up in the middle of the night and check on Jimmy in his crib. Sometimes he was asleep, but other times he just lay there, awake and quiet. When she found him like that, she picked him up, changed his diaper, and then rocked him until he drifted back to sleep.

"You must get pretty tired with carrying that baby around all the time," I said to Lucille one Sunday.

Lucille smiled and said, "I do, but it's okay."

On the fifth Sunday after Jimmy had been placed in Lucille's home, she took him to church with her as usual. The other two children, comfortable now in the church nursery, went there during the service, but as she'd done each Sunday, Lucille took Jimmy with her to the sanctuary.

I was well into my sermon when I heard something and stopped talking. In the abrupt quiet, a little cry could be heard, and when we turned to look, we saw Lucille, with a big smile on her face and tears pouring out of her eyes. But the crying sound wasn't coming from her; it came from the bundle she held in her arms.

Eileen, who was sitting next to Lucille, stared as the little boy took a deep breath and started crying louder. Finally Eileen could contain herself no longer, and in an action unusual for us quiet Methodists, she exclaimed, "Praise God."

At that, the entire congregation broke into an enthusiastic applause — probably the first time in history that worshipers have clapped *because* a child cried in church.

Later in the week, I stopped over at Lucille's. There on a blanket on the floor, was Jimmy, clucking and smiling as he played with Lucille's 5-year-old.

"You're not holding him," I observed to Lucille.

"Oh, I still hold him plenty," Lucille said, "but he seems to want some time to play now."

Easter was two weeks away. In terms of Christian theology, it's the most important day of the year. Since I'd been at North Doncaster for five Easters already, I'd been wondering what I could possibly preach about the meaning of Resurrection that I hadn't already.

But that afternoon at Lucille's, I knew.

I *knew*.

Afterword

As they now stand, the stories in this volume are works of fiction, but each one was suggested by a real event I witnessed or participated in over the course of my ministry. During that time, I have been privileged to be among people who allowed me to share their hopes and hurts, who invited me to officiate at their cheerings and at their mournings, who sat under my preaching but who often taught me as much about faith and grace as I taught them about doctrine and religion. And so, while these stories are not exactly their stories in every detail, they could have been, for incidents similar to these occur with some regularity in the small parishes that are the frontline of the church universal.

Specifically these stories could not have been imagined or written had people of the following Ohio United Methodist parishes not accepted me as their pastor and welcomed me into their lives: Cherry Valley-Williamsfield Churches, Kirkpatrick-Claridon Churches, Gustavus Federated Church, Youngstown Trinity Church, Bellevue Seybert Church, Waynesburg Centenary Church.

My appreciation and thanks to two fellow writers who read this book in its formative stages and offered invaluable suggestions: Wayne Vinson and Rebecca Purdum (who is both a writer and my daughter).

And finally, to Jeanine, who has shared all those parsonages with me and contributed in uncountable ways to the joy of the journey.

Stan Purdum